About the Author

Kay Schornstheimer was born in 1982 in Mainz/Germany.

His first short stories he published on his author blog "PULP LETTERS" that existed from 2008 till 2014.

His first novel DOPE69 has been released in 2011 by BoD.

Besides his work as an author, he is in the Rhine-Main area / Germany, a famous DJ in the local rock scene.

Kay Schornstheimer

Who are you?

Psychological Thriller

Bibliographical information of the German National Library:

The Deutsche Nationalbibliothek lists this publication in the German national bibliography; detailed bibliographic data are available on the Internet about Http://dnb.d-nb.de.

© 2016 by Kay Schornstheimer

2. Edition 2016

Manufacture & Publisher: BoD™ – Books on Demand, Norderstedt

Editing & Record: Sanela Bilalic

Printed in Germany
ISBN: 978-3-8423-8458-3

The Act and all characters appearing in this work are fictitious. Any similarity to persons, living or dead, or actual events is entirely coincidental.

For

João Carlos (Mr. White) Oliveira Matos

Based on the short story:

Das Handy

By Kay Schornstheimer, published in 2008 on
www.pulp-letters.com

For

Frank (called) Bongartz

Sometimes I wish I am taking a sharp carpet knife and putting it between my big toe and the one next to it. Then I am pulling it out hard and slipping it through to the end.

I dream of unfolding myself from my shelf and slipping away.

Finally free and untroubled!

Great idea, isn´t it?

Searching for Help

I am standing in front of Rita's door.

I need her help, but I think I will not knock.

But what alternatives do I have?

My best friend is dead; there are no other friends left.

I have no siblings.

And my parents? Forget them!

I do not have anyone.

Rita and I are not together for more than four months. We broke up on good terms. I accepted her desire of separation without making a problem out of it. We know each other from our childhood onwards, and she could always rely on me.

So why would not she help me?

"Overcome it, and do it finally" I say to myself.

Now!

I must do it. Just do it - damn it, do it!

I knock. Rita opens the door, we look at each other, and she closes the door again.

"Go away, Dirk!" she screams through the closed door.

I did not imagine our meeting will be like this, but I cannot blame her for that. I would also do the same at the first moment.

"Come on, let me in Rita… I beg you! "Go or I will call the police!" she screams hysterically.

"Why the police?"

"Do you want to muck me around?"

An eligible question, I have to admit. I cannot give her a reason why should not she call the police.

But she could at least listen to me and what I have to say.

"That was not me! Please believe me!"

"You went and left him lying there. Do you know that they will find you? The Criminal Investigation Department came to me and asked about you."

So far, the investigation on me looks like this: they have already checked out my past. They know all the details about my life. Which school I have attended, what is my occupation, who are my friends, what my relationship status is, how much

money do I have on my account, whether I got speeding ticket, simply everything. I feel exposed. "I was tricked. You have to believe me! I am innocent! Could I otherwise come here?"
She does not say anything.
"Rita, I do not know where I should go. You are the only one who can help me." After I had made this statement, I immediately realized that it is the truth. I know that it is my last chance to prove my innocence.
I am making a break to carefully think about what I should say next. At the same moment, the door behind me is opening. One of Rita's neighbors is coming in the hallway from her apartment. It is Mrs. Schneider, an elderly lady who has already reached the age of retirement and lives alone. I know her more or less by sight from the time I was living there. Rita does not like her because she has always complained about alleged noise and other things.
"What in God´s name is going on here, what does this mean?" she rumbles.
I became angry and before turning around I moved my hands from Rita's door.
"Fuck you bitch, before I tear your head off and puke in your neck!" I shouted at Rita's neighbor. Shocked from what I told her, she immediately went back to her apartment. I hear she locked the door twice and put the chain on the door.
"And what are you expecting from me now, to let you in? “ Rita asks me. Although she probably

liked this play with her neighbor. But even I am shocked by my aggressiveness. I do not actually act like that at all.

"Shit ..."I curse quietly to myself. I turn back to her apartment door.

"Simply go, Dirk, disappear from here!"

"You know that I didn't do it, you know me. You told me I am your favorite guy in the world, and I have never done something that disapproves it."

This sentence brings a moment of silence.

"Let me please in, and I will tell you everything about what actually happened."

"You want to talk about it?"

"Yes."

"Then start talking. But you are not going to cross the door, it is clear"!

"And your neighbor"?

"I do not care".

"You cannot let me in? " I implore her to note how uncomfortable to me it is to stand here.

"You are trying in vain, Dirk," she says with a mixture of fear and anger in her voice.

I sat down with my back against her door and leaned on it.

"Are you going to start talking soon?"

I can clearly understand that she rejects me. And I cannot even blame her. Care from her side is the last thing is can expect now. The man she used to know is wiped out because of the recent events. She was taken to a vague memory that had never corresponded to the truth. This new image that she has about me, is the same as that of an evil monster. She finds everything overwhelming, even listening to me but she refuses any kind of escape. She is a prisoner in her own apartment. In her small two-room apartment, without balcony, on the third floor. She cannot even jump from the window without being seriously hurt by falling on cemented floor. Despite the last option she is left with, namely to call the police, she does nothing. Instead, she throws me a bone in the form of a small chance to prove her that I am really innocent. But rather of being grateful to her, I get even more angry and frustrated by her behavior.

"It is OK ... God!" The anger in my voice can only make the situation worse. I would like to jump and cross her door. But it would make the image of evil monster even stronger. Thus I decide to continue talking and, if possible, to sound resignedly. "It was on Thursday, and everything has started with my cellphone."

"With your cellphone?" she asks confused.

"Yes, with my cellphone. Please shut up now and listen to me." I am still irritated and annoyed, but in a quieter tone of voice just to make her know that I don´t want to be interrupted.

"So it was Thursday and ..."

Incorrectly connected
(How it all happened...)

Dennis comes for a visit, we spend our time
drinking alcohol, smoking dope and playing
Angry Birds.
And we pose important questions to ourselves:
Is Elvis still alive, and if yes, is he in nursing
center?
Was Jesus black?
Who is Gobi Todic?
Is the number forty-two really the answer to
everything?

Is there already a fixed day when everything will
be over?
What does Osama Bin Laden do today, after his
fake death?
When will be Mario Gomez finally emerged from
the German national eleven thrown?
When will Prosieben finally stop emitting terrible
sets *Galileo*? And why do they constantly repeat
the same episodes of *How I
Met Your Mother* and *the Big Bang Theory*?
And is it really always the same? Actually
everything is made in repeating circuit?

After a while Dennis decides to go. He has an
important meeting tomorrow. It is a large order
from IBM, he has to be fit and to get enough sleep.
I bring him to the door and wish him good luck for
tomorrow. After I had closed the door, I heard his
cellphone ringing in the corridor outside. I am
tired at once, I see black spots in front of my eyes
and only thing I can do is to go to bed. There I fall
directly into a deep sleep.

Three to four hours later...

I wake up with the song *Break Out* by *Foo Fighters*.
Where does it come from?
From my cellphone. I look at the clock next to my
bed: few minutes after two o´clock - early in the
morning.
Who the hall calls me at this time?

I am angrily taking my cellphone.
"Who is it?"
"Hello," says a quiet voice on the other side of pipe.
"Tell me, you Depp, do you know how late it is ...
Who is that at all?"
"Who is that?" asks the voice.
"I am not interested in such games after you woke
me up." I look to the display of my phone which
shows Dennis´s name.
"Dennis, what is this shit?"
"Here is not Dennis."
"Yes, funny," I say annoyed and hang up.
It rings again.
I go back to it.
"Tell me, Dennis, is it because of your excitement
about tomorrow, or are you so drunk?"
"Here is not Dennis", claims the caller same as few
minutes ago.
Who could be that otherwise? His friend? No, it
cannot be. He doesn´t have any other friends. He
has told me last evening that he cannot stay longer
since he has to sleep in order to be relaxed for
tomorrow. And now, he calls in the middle of the
night with a strange voice. He changed it so that I
cannot recognize him, but I did in the end. And
yeah, he calls from his phone number without
making it invisible. Well my friend, that is stupid.
"And why do you call then from your phone
number?"
"Because I found it."

Good answer, I have to admit. But I am still quite annoyed by this situation and my tiredness makes the thing even worse. But I would still like to sleep now, it is very late, damn it. Before I answer him I breathe deeply.
"You have found the cellphone?" I have asked quietly but then I said: "Stop Dennis, it is enough!"
"I am not fucking Dennis, damn!" he screams and sounds very angry, although I am the one who has the right to behave like that. Taken aback, I light a cigarette.
"And who are you?" I ask him but I stay bored still.
"Ben. Ok, I am Ben".
I am taking a short break to see whether I know someone called Ben, who may be under the quilt together with Dennis, making his stupid joke call.
"So you are Ben and you have found the mobile phone of my friend Dennis. So, what do you want from me now?"
"Your number was last dialed."
"And this is why are you calling me now, right?"
"Yes."
"Well ... you know what, you will get his fixed-line number from me and you can call him tomorrow to see how you can give him his cellphone back ", I say it to him while I am opening a bottle of water standing next to my bed and taking a drink.
"Do you know where I had found the phone?" he asks.
"No," I answer.
"Why?"

"Because I want to sleep."
"I have found it in the staircase, directly in front of
my apartment door."
"I'm not interested."
"Why?"
"Tell me, do you want to muck me or what. I have
already said that I want to sleep, haven´t I? Did
you perhaps come up with the idea that the owner
of the cellphone lives in your house? If you have
found it in the Staircase – an idea only."
He: "No, he does not live here. I know everyone
from the floor and there is no one called Dennis"
"Do you have something to write with? Or shall I
send you his fixed-line number via SMS?"
"You and Dennis are good friends?"
My conversation partner is slowly becoming
angry. Now I am totally pissed.
"You are getting on my nerves, man. What do you
want from me?"
"Honestly, I do not know either."
"What an asshole" I say to myself, holding the
phone a bit far away.
"Do you want his fixed-line number? Yes or No?"
"I do not believe that he can use it now?"
"What should it mean? Did you put it in your ass
or wink on it?"
"No. He does not look like being able to use it."
This statement makes me speechless. A
spontaneous confusion spreads inside of me, and I
get a strange feeling in the stomach.

"Hello is anyone there?" asks Ben in a striking quiet tone.

"What?" I asked carefully. "You have just told me that you found it, have not you?"

"That's true."

"Well, I'm not still getting your point?"

"Well, saying that I found the cellphone is not entirely true." He makes a pause. "I got it lifted after he dropped it."

I get a goose skin and the strange feeling in my stomach became stronger.

"Ahh, and… Did you see him dropping it, or how it happened?"

"Close."

"And why you did not say to him."

"That was not possible."

"Why?"

"I guess, after I was done with him, he simply did not have enough strength to do anything," he sounds a little weird and brings me once again to silence.

"You are joking me, or what?"

"Why should I do, Dirk?"

My adrenaline shoots in the height.

"Wait, how do you know my name? Dennis saved my number under *defective with O R* in his phonebook"

"He has told me ... shortly before I have cut his vocal cords."

"What have you done? Where is he?" I am gasping
on the phone. The fear overcomes me so much that
I felt petrified. Like a deer in the headlights.
"He is in front of your door."
I run to the door and open it. Dennis is located
directly in front of my door with slotted throat. In
a huge blood pool which seeps into the carpet.
There is a pattern of blood splashes on the
wallpaper and my door. Shocked by seeing this,
everything inside me gets frozen. Dennis´s face is
congealed into a pale, bloody nightmare. I stare
into the dark hole of his wide-open mouth over the
gash on his neck. He has his eyes wide open. He is
completely expressionless staring into the infinite
void. I got sweaty all over my back. I cannot look
away, even if I want to. I cannot even control it, I
search for something in his face – for anything.
Despair, terror, disbelief - but none of these is to be
seen in those empty, cold eyes.
I am alone here and rigid stunned from the lifeless
body of my best friend. I cannot simply believe
what I see. I would like to believe that it was only a
bad dream and that I will wake up every moment.
But I cannot wake up, because this is not a dream.
I lose control over my legs and I fall to the ground.
My back gets hurt by the door pillar. The pain
extends all over my body. The phone is still in my
hand. After a while I notice that he is still on the
call saying *Hello*. I put the phone on my ear again.
"Well, do you like what you see?" the guy, called
Ben, asks me.

"You sick wanker, what have you done to him!" I shout.
"Dirk, listen to me."
"Fuck you!"
"Dirk, your mobile phone is out of power."
"What?"
"Dirk, you are speaking with yourself all the time"
"What?"
"Well, who is now the sick wanker?"
"What?"
"Good night, killer".

Powerless

I wake up in my car.

I need a moment to come back to myself.
After a while, I realize what actually has
happened. The ongoing from few hours ago meets
me like a flash. I get a flashback in front of my
eyes.
The evening with Dennis.
The call in the middle of the night.
The strange person called Ben on the other side of
the line of my cellphone, or better to say on the
other side of the radio signal.
The dead body of Dennis in front of my door.

My entertaining collapse.
And the run away.
Yes, I ran away. With fear. With fear from that
what happened. From that what is inevitably
going to happen.
I just wanted to go, go away from my apartment.
Out of Mainz.
I went into my car and drove to where people from
Mainz are not willing to go:
In the direction of Wiesbaden.
The trip did not last long. After almost ten minutes
of driving I stopped at the place *Zur alten Römer
Straße* on the road A671 and parked there.
I was so exhausted that I fell asleep few minutes
later.
And now here I am.
The dawn has already begun and the chirping of
birds drives me in the madness. There are still a
few stars to see on the purple colored sky and it is
foggy. After I had lit a cigarette and two deep
trains inhaled, I switch the radio on. I listen to the
Song *Fear Is a Place To Live* by *Korn* and I am trying
not to think about anything.
But my cellphone does not let me in peace.
It rings again.
The number of Dennis is shown on the display. I
feel scared while taking it but I hope that
everything is only a stupid joke. Dennis made a
deal with someone to fool me and now wants to
explain everything. Please God, let it happen!
I answer the call.

"Hello Dirk."
I immediately recognize the voice. That is Ben.
I scream angrily in my phone:
"You wanker, you miserable piece of shit, what did you do with Dennis?"
"Calm down", says the voice.
»Asshole! If I catch you, I'll kill you! Who are you cursed? Tell me! Who are you? «
"Here is no one called Ben, I have already told you"
»Who are you? «
» You should rather ask yourself this question. Yes! Honestly speaking, what you are doing at the moment? «
» What? Damn what's your name? «
"My name is Dirk. Just like you, because I am you."
"Listen to him!"
"Do not be frustrated, Dirk. It would be better if you quickly clear it to yourself and admit that you are the one who make these calls."
"What the shit is all this about?"
"Your phone is still not on."
I do not say anything; breathing is now a difficult task for me. I am trying to calm down, but it does not work. I have the feeling that my throat knots and that I am about to choke. It is very hot here and I feel beads of sweat on my forehead. My hands start to sweat so strong that it is taking my effort away and I am not able to hold the mobile phone. What actually I need to do. I cannot hear the voice anymore.

"If it is so difficult for you to accept the truth, you can continue to pretend that you are talking to the mysterious voice, which has lured you into a trap. It does not matter, I am fine with that. "
The language is devious, and also the voice gets quitter. I enjoy the suddenly occurred silence as never before in my life. What for a sick person is he? He wants me to believe that we are the same person? Should I believe in this shit? I am not a psycho. I could never kill someone, and certainly not my best friend. And I am not calling myself while sitting in the car. I have talked to myself as a child but that was for fun, just like every other kid does. There is nothing strange or sick about it.

What for a sick game is this and who is this guy? His voice and his way of talking seems known to me, almost familiar. But I cannot identify it. This leads to only one conclusion: I have met him before for sure.

"I have a surprise for you" the voice tells to me.
"Take a look in your suitcase space."
"No!" I shout and hang up.
It rings again. I do not want to answer it. I try to resist, but something obliges me to do it - and I cannot go against that.
"What do you want from me?" I would like to know from the voice.
"I want you to look in your luggage compartment. Now!"

"What?"
"We do not have time for this shit. Just do it!"
"Leak me!"
"Well, do it!" says the voice.
"OK", I shout and strike against the steering wheel at the same time.
I go out of the car to the boot. I am in front of it and thinking about what I will find there. It can be anything. Something that can bring me even more problems? I do not open it. I play with my thoughts of throwing the cellphone away and leaving. But what is it? What is inside? He said it is a surprise? A surprise in the sense of something good? Possibly it is something that would end this nightmare and would give me courage to open it. Then I simply said: "Fuck it!" and I opened the cursed cover of the luggage compartment.
I am making make few steps back after seeing what is inside it.
"Oh God," I whisper quietly in shock.
Before I dare to get closer to it, I first look around to be sure I am alone here and that no one is watching. It is a young woman huddled in my luggage compartment. She is certainly not older than twenty. Street-style blond hair and blue eyes wide open, same like the ones from Dennis, staring into the blank space. Her mouth is open a little as well. On the forehead - near the right temple – is a swollen wound, and beside it a bloody stone.

"Na, killer, do you like what you see?" a wicked giggle interrupts the voice asking: "Do you have already overcome the shock?"

"Fuck! Who is that?"

"How should I know? Obviously, a bitch."

"She is really dead?" I ask in a childlike and naive sound.

"Dead just like Dennis."

"What have you done?"

"That was not me. That was you.”

"Do not say that shit again!"

"I am saying only the truth."

"And what do you think when I could do this?"

"While you were sleeping, actually while you were thinking you are sleeping. You haven´t not slept for couple of months." He makes a short break before he continues: "You have hit her with a stone."

"I did not kill anyone!"

"I did," he tells me indifferent to the answer and then asks me: "What do we do now?"

"What do you mean with *what do we do now*? I call the police now, asshole, it is enough!"

"Do not do it! We are not going to like it. Our lives are embodied in one soul." His voice sounds mercilessly.

"What do you mean by *us*?"

"Shut up and listen!" warns Ben´s voice. "The body is in your car and you will be probably suspected of killing your so-called best friend. It does not bring anything good to you. Do you seriously

think that the cups will believe you a single word?
Do not be so naive."
"But ..."
The voice interrupts me. "No but ... The question
you have to answer now is how to get out of the
thing again? The one with Dennis you cannot
deny, mainly because you disappeared. You might
say you suffer from spiritual illness. What is the
truth? But so far there is no reason to blame you
for the dead woman in your trunk. You have to
disappear!"
"Oh God, help me, what should I do?" I ask
myself.
The bad thing is that Ben is right. This is clear to
me at this moment. The murder of Dennis is
attributed to me and I do not know if I ever can
prove the contrary. At least not at this moment.
And now this strange corpse in my car! What
should I do? To call the police and say "Look, that
was not me"? They would immediately punch me
and never let me go. And this asshole, who made
this all to me, is gone long ago. Damn! He puts me
in the corner, and is not letting me out anymore.
I want to calm the thoughts in my head. Why me?
Why does Ben play this game with me? I have to
do everything he says. I have no other choice. I am
powerless against that voice.
"You can do this, Dirk. You just need to keep a
clear mind and to follow my instructions."
"What do you think I should do? " I ask the voice.

"You have to disappear so that they cannot blame you for this murder. Another person has to be brought into connection with it."
I would never come to this idea alone without this *Sherlock Holmes* who is hiding behind the voice – I think ironically.
"Understood, and what next?"
"Let it looks like a rape with subsequent homicide. Take her and the weapon to the forest and tear her clothes. No fear! There won´t be any fingerprint left nor DNA particles on the stone and fabrics. The rain will wash them away, at least I believe in it. Just make it sure that no one sees you putting her in a blanket. And hurry up!"
I follow his instructions. I have no blanket in my car. Thus I put her in the car seat cover. I leave her body about two kilometers away from the car park in the adjacent forest on the highway. I tear her black top and then the black slip too, which I put beside her. I place the bloody stone right next to her skull.
The phone rings again.
"Well, it was not so difficult?"
"Oh, fuck yourself! " I say full of disgust.
"Do not use such bad words, young man, I am trying to help you."
"You are helping me not to laugh?"
"One more thing you have to do."
"What?"
"Fuck her."
"What?"

"It should look like a rape with corresponding injury. So go ahead, blow it with her and be brutal, so that everything is comprehensible. But do not forget to use a condom so that you leave no traces. And do not forget to throw the condom and the coatings away."

"Forget it!"

"Go ahead, that is your opportunity, it is meant to you. "

"Anything else?"

"I have to admit that if she is still warm and a bit damp, it would make you more fun, but in the situation in which you are now, you do not have a choice. It will also reduce the stress you have, before you completely freak out. "

"This cannot be true? Damn! "

"Now fuck the dead piece of meat", he urges me.

"You are sick! "

"Yes, I am, and I am also your mirror image. "

"What? "

"Now hold your stupid mouth closed and make it work. You do not want to stay on your own way?"

"I will not do it!"

"Now fuck her! We do not have time."

"No, I will not!"

"Do it!"

"No!"

"Go now!"

"Never!"

"Do it now!"

"No fucking way"

"Well, then I will do it."

"What?"

42

Escape

I wake up beside dead woman who was lying in my luggage compartment lag. I think I have fainted.
What is going on here?
I am naked and a semen-filled condom is on my penis.
I did it! But how is this possible?
I feel bad.
My only wish is to get away from here.
I tear the rubber from me and get dressed. I drive two kilometers with my car. In the meantime I was driving throughout the place with the dead body

in it. When I arrived, I was completely out of breath, but I did not have time to take a rest and I moved immediately on.
Just to go away from here.
I am driving from the A671 onto the A66 in the direction of Frankfurt. I find a pack of cigarettes in the glove compartment and smoke chain of it. I am now for more an hour away. Frankfurt is already behind me. I do not know where I am at the moment and it does not matter. Other traffic participants, traffic signs with the prescribed speed and warning signs such as gradients, slope, curves, panels, the next exit, or signs with mileage to the nearest petrol station or with frequencies from here receivable radio transmitters noise, I have passed without considering them.
I am getting calmed now and starting to sort the thoughts and experiences in my head.
But unsuccessfully.
A big fat question mark is in my head. How could I get myself in all this mess? It is incomprehensible to me since I always stay away from any trouble.
I always left when the others started fighting in the school. Sometimes I was involved in one fight but I have never been the one who began the fight.
Except for the one time. It was clearly a physical torture. I hit a guy with my leg and he fell down to the stoneground. He spread some evil rumors about me, which were wrong. I believe that he told my friends he saw me talking to myself on the cellphone, or anything of that sort.

Shortly after that happened, I was sorry for what I did and I had a sleepless night. The following morning when I arrived at the school, I was looking to talk directly to him and to apologize for my behavior. Until this incident, I have never done something similar to anyone, and no one could say anything against me. Uninterested in this story, my cellphone rings again. It shows on the display again the number of Dennis. This time I do not believe that everything will turn out good. I know who is at the other side of the line and that he will not let me in peace until I accept the call and let him say, what he has to say to me. So I answer the call.

"When I catch you, I will kill you", is the first thing I hear from him. That surprised and scared me. The words I have just said, coupled with the accompanying feeling of pure hatred and disgust, are now new to me.

"Yes, suicide would be a solution in your case, or listen to me from now on and there will not be more errors."

I do not know what I should say, never mind, and do not pay attention to the meaning of this statement. The indifference to this saying makes me unwilling to clear it. I do not think I need an answer.

"You forgot something regarding your dead playmate."

"Fuck you, you know?" I feel out of energy right now. My level of tolerance is already exceeded.

What actually wants this guy from me - what should I have forgotten? My mind? Would this be something? I guess that I had already lost it long ago, but now I only need to reverse and take it back. It lies somewhere here. Somewhere near my "dead playmate". I clutch the steering wheel and see, how my face expression has derailed into a cynical resigned laugh. Since I am traveling eighty kilometers per hour, my head falls gradually forward the cool imitation leather, with which the handlebar is coated. My heart is beating so hard into the steering wheel so that it demolishes the worn pommel of the gear.

"Can you hear me at all? You have made a serious mistake."

"And what? What damn it? What I was supposed to do, you piece of shit?"

"The condom, that you have not taken with ... congratulations you have left your DNA, a best peace of proof. You will now be attributed to this crime. Can you do anything properly?", asks me the voice of contempt.

You cannot make anything properly? I hate this sentence! It accompanies me during my whole life. Again and again I get to listen to this. From my stepfather, my teachers, and from my training manager in my apprenticeship as professional. No matter what I did - it was always wrong! It was incorrect or could be made better or … it cursed again everything - but it was never correct. May all of them braise in hell!

I feel how nausea hits me again.
I need a rest.
My left hand moves to the blinker, but I let it fall again. The last thing I need now is a hamburger gaffer, for each "newcomer" something like a cinema event on a canvas. All idlers - who know everything better than you! Traitors! They are all traitors - just like: Hello corpses' abusers! We do see everything! Bite our citizen and we know your fucking past! Severe childhood? Of course we can see you on the nose tip!
 I want to go to the resting place now. I want to scream in the face of the next newcomer "go somewhere else and watch what people are doing there, you rubbish hypocrites! " I would like to watch how your bloody grin disappears as you leave all together, same way the woman of the band guy says: "Get out of here! He is crazy! "
 Exactly!
Crazy! That is what I am. You are right. And as I move toward her, I unpack my penis, but this time without a condom. This time I will do it right, as Ben's voice wants it from me". I want to pick up my jacket, which is located in the luggage compartment, and to execute the burger eaters. And then I would like to make them whimpering, oh yes! I want it.
Murder delight!
There is already a long standstill. Where is the next comment of the omniscient? Ben waits for something new? Did he ask anything while I was

watching the movie in my head, and I did not hear? Can I finally make anything correctly? Exactly - this was his problem. His...
But why? How does he know all this?
The resting place is behind me. The fat, lucky people and their dung girlfriends. They may have a bit of their life now. And not to be ashamed of me. What a waste of...
"How *do* you know all this?" I whisper in my cell phone. I hear my own voice. I can feel how each word seeps into the ground in an unfathomable black space in the middle of my head. And now I shout - like a madman before he experiences his own nervous breakdown: "are you watching me, you pig manure?"
I am starting to sweat. The welding is in my eyes. Let me for a moment forget my nausea. I wipe it with the right sleeve way, as good as I can. I press my eyelids together several times. Now I can see a little clearer again. My right hand rests on the steering wheel back. The car is already above the right boundary strip, I draw it back into the track. It seems like he wants to tell me: Hello, I am your limit strip! Not *just any* boundary strip, but - exactly - you! Of course, stupid, I am not unto this - perhaps it is the other way around - but I can show you something. That is vicinity. A vicinity to the crash barrier, the vicinity to the accident, the vicinity to your end. Well, but you could also be lucky. Perhaps you would have only few scratches - or your car would have few scratches. Then were

the scratches on the crash barrier the witness of your past - the scratches on your car as well. But they are nothing - absolutely NOTHING - compared to the scratches on the crash barrier! Because they will remain. They remain as a corpse, somewhere behind you in high grass. But the scratches on you – pardon, on your car - they are what really counts. They are what is interesting. You are colorless, and they show the raw plate, but at the guardrail - branded legacy of your miserable fate - you can see your color. Your sperm. And then they will be looking after you. They will follow. Hunting you. As long as you are finally brought to the track, and why?

Why? I start to freeze, I am shaking so much, and the following question is shaking me as well: what can I do if I cannot shake off this block on my leg, this fucking piece of evidence. Why? Because I cannot make anything. Because I could never really listen what others are saying to me? Because I miss the boundary strips. Because I always forget that there is *only one* who knows everything about me and has me in his hand and tastes me served like a puppet? But how can he do this? *How* can Ben do all this to me?

I notice that the radio is turned on. It must be playing all the time, but I have not noticed. Perhaps I forgot that it is playing the whole time. Very quiet, but still hearable. It is Pixies station and they ask a question: *Where is my mind?* -it fits somehow.

I am freezing even more now. Ice-cold showers are running all over my back. I start automatically to look in the rear-view mirror. Is someone following me? The rear bench seat is empty, as well as the road. There is no one on the speeding road. Only dark and mysterious emptiness is what is concealed. It runs after me, hunting me to let me know where I am. *Someone*? Or *he*? He - the lurking man in my mobile phone, from whose vocal cord, blood freezes- to remind me where I was and what I did. He watches me. It cannot be other way around. I sweat even more, watching to the darkness of the night. I repeat my last question. Only in my head.
And I receive a reply.
"Of course I see you all the time, because we are after all ..."
I should like to suspend Ben before he finish the sentence: "Listen, I told you that we are not the same person, you just want to blame me for everything, and this is just a case of ..."
Now he interrupts me.
"A huge conspiracy? Like for the *X-files* or *chuck*? Or from any TV series, you have watched?"
"If it helps you, then look to me but simply as to your dark companion, like in the soap opera *Dexter*."
This answer brings me to the silence. The words that I have just heard penetrate from the distant past of a long forgotten dream in my consciousness. As creeping venom, gradually

dropped from a wad of cotton wool sheds into my thoughts. I feel myself paralyzed during the blank area of the street which flew behind me. The infinity of the whole universe, like a mockery limited by side strips, I am crossing right now. I stare out into the frenetic emptiness. I feel like it invites me to become part of it. The boundary line taunts me to drive over it. Is there the infinity because it is always somewhere in us? In me?
I would like to get out of my body just for a while, to get rid of my thoughts.
How does this asshole know what for series I watch? Why do I have never noticed that? He is from the NSA? Or has the ISIS fingers in the game? Maybe he has hidden cameras and bugs them in my apartment. Oh God, please let it was the case, and let the police find them when they search my apartment so that they realize that something is rotten in the whole thing and that I am not the killer, but only the supposed scapegoat.
My gaze falls on the fuel display. Only a quarter of it is left, it will not last long and I have to find a tank station. I can drive few miles more. But not forever.
Forever - what a word. How long is *forever*?
Perhaps the road limit knows more about this? It has actually a beginning or an end? Or does it ends again in it at the end? A raging, white bow to propel its viewers into madness...
For a moment I am thinking of going home, to see if the police are perhaps already arrived. It would

be enough fuel in the tank. Maybe I can still forestall the police and track down the bugs and cameras? Maybe …

My gaze on the fuel gauge is falling further. Red button starts easily to pulsate. At the same time it seems as if it would somehow lose its shape. My view is deflected by it, focuses downright obsessively on something else. The vibrant red of the needle is completely reversed.

And suddenly I know instantly why.

I put the phone in my lap and look at my hands. I hold no longer the steering wheel firmly. I keep them with widely separated fingers spread before me. A bright red condom is inverted around each finger. Blood is under each of them. In the background I hear a barely perceptible noise - the hum of cameras. Are they actually modern mini cameras? The condoms pull suddenly making my fingers hot while the blood still oozes through crack out of my skin. The condoms pumps located on my fingers are slowly but steadily getting bigger and bigger. I turn my hands so that I can see from the inner side.

Something is missing!

I am seeking in vain for the lifeline.

But it is not the only thing missing here. The skin on both hands is completely smooth. I fall into panic and try to tear the condom from my right index finger, but I slip again on its smooth, vibrant surface. Smooth? Completely smooth! So smooth my skin is!

No lifeline.
As red as the needle.
No…
Fingerprints!
The condom over my right index finger bursts. I
look to the natural creases in my skin, everything
is covered with blood, and I cannot see anything.
What if the cameras and bugs are littered with my
own fingerprints?
I try helplessly to calm down. But once it was
silent, the cry of new, much more serious thoughts
rises up in me. What if there were no fingerprints?
It would be just the same if there am absolutely
only me. I would … just follow the line. The white
line on the road, exploded in front of my eyes in a
dazzling white, as if it comes from burning
napalm. I tear my hands up and plump with my
right bottom against the steering wheel. A shrill
sound rips my thoughts and leaves darkness in the
white flow, while an ardent pain from my right
hand shoots up to the shoulder. I see in my eyes
how the right guardrail, against whom I am
standing, goes away from me. The sound that has
been interrupted is close to my left ear now; a
white flash shoots out from the side mirrors in the
direction of me and starts to blind. Something
huge misses me. The wind rushes like the violent
dead breath against the side of my car, and I step
involuntarily out. But it is hardly noticeable. I
stand on the spot in the middle of the roadway.

In front of my windshield, I can see the taillights of the truck, which nearly rammed me and now stops. I realize what happened. My foot had slipped off the accelerator, and I have not notice anything. I am standing in the middle of the right lane of the highway. I have luck that there is no traffic, otherwise I would be already a strip of blood and sheet metal too.

At one stroke, I wake up from my daydream. I light the dead engine and do not pay attention to the truck drivers, but simply give full throttle to get away as quickly as possible from here. A moment later, I head to the side panels, and move as gently as possible until me to the car. I put off the engine and sit perfectly rigid. I look down at my hands. They are deathly pale and trembling so much that I do not manage to bring them to rest. I'm freezing and sweating at the same time, the power is soaked from my legs. I open the window down let the fresh air, clear air into the interior of my vehicle. I take deep breath in and out, again and again. After half an hour I have the feeling that everything is perfect with me. I notice that my phone has been dropped from my lap into the footwall of the car. I did not have it during the drive? I think so. Maybe I should do it again in the future if I do not want again to stray from the road. It is not prohibited without reason, to take a call while driving... I put my left hand down and search for my mobile phone. It is slipped between the seat and the floor. With pointed fingers, I pull

it out and look at the display. It is turned off, the screen is blue, and I press a key. With whom I had actually spoken?
I started to laugh to myself. With whom I had spoken? Is not it interesting? I'm still alive, and that is what really counts, or?
On the screen of my mobile phone appears blue color as it switches to standby mode.
I am alive, no matter how and no matter where. And that is the only thing that counts.
What do I complain against?
The display of my mobile phone flames light blue and I hear a ring tone. The number of Dennis is on the display. I put it to my left ear.
I hear a voice. A well-known voice. The voice of Ben.

About what are you complaining about? Your life was the pure boredom before, and now it's finally really starting, as in your favorite series. "

I have actually managed it for a moment, to forget completely the voice, and was in faith that every-thing is OK. That was not the incident. I survived, and I can live normally now.

"Why cannot you just leave me alone" I ask the voice.

"Why should I? Since I'm here, you feel for the first time that you are alive. Only now, when your ex-perienced ridiculous near-crash. And I am not talk-ing about your anxiety, you become like that when you're exposed to a confrontation of such kind. Do not you realize that it is different this time? And you like it secretly? But you deny it and do not want to admit it. Why? "

"Give me finally rest," I implore him. I sneak my eyes tightly together and a tear is running down my cheek.

"Why, because I'm right?"

"I do not care!" I say while I open my tearful eyes.

"Dirk, you need me."

"Oh?" I say, and throw the phone out of the car. I hastily close the window, start the engine and step on the accelerator.

"Finally rest."

And now...?

I park on a rest stop, shortly before the Kassel.

I sit in my car and enjoy the peace and stay quiet
while I'm watching the action on the service area
and smoking my last cigarette. The radio is on, and
the windows are closed. I manage to ignore the
noise, that penetrates from outside.
I need a plan. A good plan with which I can
manage to clear up everything and to prove my
innocence. If they find me, it's going to be too late;
they will not believe a word I say and will lock me
away. I need to get rid of my car, they are already
searching for it. There is also no fuel in it, and since
I forgot my wallet in my apartment, I do not have

any other option. Well, except the almost ten euros, which I have found in my car. Instead of investing the few euros in gasoline, I'd better eat something and maybe it's enough even for a box of tipping. The only question is how I get out of here now, and where I should go. I need help, but from whom? Who wants to help a man who is suspected for a murder and is on the run?

I can only hope that my face or my description did not appear in the media, which would only make the situation more difficult. But where and to whom to go?

I need someone who knows me, someone who knows me for a long time, and believes that I would never be able to do something like that. Someone whom I can trust, and who is very close to me, to my thoughts and words.

The only person who comes to my mind is Rita. We were, until recently, a pair, well, she called me a liar in our last conversation, but it was about something else. Not an alleged murder I had committed. I know that she will believe me. After all, we know each other since our childhood. I still remember how we first met, it was in elementary school, I was in second grade and she in third. One day I had trouble with a fourth-grader who has stolen my eight-pack Knoppers during the long break and has thrown my entire sandwich in the dirt. I had a fear of this guy; after all, he was two heads taller than me and twice as heavy.

Nevertheless, I did not want to give up on my sandwich so easily. Although I was always silent one who has never enjoyed fighting with others, except for that one time when I decided to ask my fear. And what is also important to remember: I was hungry, damn it!

My mother sent me to bed without having a dinner the night before because I was rude to her, and I did not have breakfast because I overslept. And now this. I had full nose. Spurred by my incredible hunger, as we know, hunger can turn us into a different person; I introduced myself to him and wanted to fight. After I was but at least six times thrown in the dirt, I decided to lie and continue to starve rather than to cash in even more beatings. But then came Rita, which hit the guy in the eggs from behind. As he slumped with his head in and it sounds uttered that I had never heard before, Rita took my sandwich from him, helped me to get on my feet and gave me my food. I fell in love with her.

I did the same for her on the playground few years later, when I rescued her from drowning in the lake. Unfortunately, I have never dared to confess my love to her. And that is how we became "best friends".

The thing I was not happy about was her relationship with another gu. But I thought, "Fuck it, better than nothing." And at least I was always close to her. Since I never dare to venture any rapprochement attempts with her, she thought for a long time that I was gay.

We went through everything together, what growing up brought with itself, even if some part of it was one-sided designed. We were always there for each other, even when some guys (mostly assholes, well, almost always) left her. Or I wanted some girl in who I have actually never had interest. And then, two years ago, it happened. My dearest wish was fulfilled when I hardly reckoned:

Rita was single for a long time and I worked quite hard at that time and I could not be friend to her – I mean I didn´t have time to spend with her even though that could have an impact on our friendship.

The night before, I had been a guest at the birthday party of my work colleague. It was the middle of the week, but we had Company holiday. The only thing that was clear to me was that I want to celebrate New Year's Eve decently. It could not hurt since it was small birthday party. But it didn´t turn out as a small party in the end. Yeah! It was really big party. HUGE PARTY. Quite powerful, to be precise. And the land called "from the post", where we were celebrating, was also as vast as it was beautiful. Shortly after midnight, the first drunks were lying around in the garden. A whole battalion of gas-fired heaters giants ensured that we do not get freeze in the middle of winter. If that was not hot enough, everyone could open his/ her eyes at any time, take a look to "Party Peggy" (the olle force – Grumpy), and enjoy snacks and drink tequila from the bottle. They estimated that there was distributed one hundred to one hundred twenty kilos on a roughly one meter sixty-five large body. Almost hypnotic. As a lava lamp. My colleague took care of everything and always went back to "Corpses pouring". In any case he called it so (it was really quite a Depp) when he strode worried about people lying all over the place and conscientiously examined whether they still move their lips after they drunk a five-liter jar of Rum. Some guests have already gone, few others, mostly couples, are spread throughout the entire house. I was on a camping hammock and almost fainted when my friend placed an electroshock gun beside my ear and activated it. He did not touch me with that thing, but the sharp, loud buzz let me boot five seconds off my lethargy. My colleague collapsed on the swing next to me. On the other side of the outdoor was a table full with the alcoholic stuff "Party Peggy". The thing was enormously huge. I registered everything through a thick, highly concentrated mist, while my laughter reflex drowned in the moment when he tried to break the web. My colleague went over to the compost tub and poured surge straw rum into it. He stared for a while in the tub, then looked over at me, then back into the vat, nodded and returned again to me and the swings. I surprisingly looked at his face while he was bringing me the Rumkaraffe. The huge

Rumkaraffe. I cannot remember whether I drunk it all. The last thing I remember is that I woke up in my bed the other morning. I think I took a cub. I see yellow lights and something soft. Something soft, but so big. Downright enormous. My Skull growled, as if it had been edited with a jackhammer. I pressed both palms against my forehead. I grimaced as I rubbed and simultaneously pressed. It was awful.
I stretched out both arms to the ceiling. My shoulder joints cracked, as if they were made of rotten wood.
Terrible!
But long not as atrocious as the clapping. When I put my right arm down, I felt huge pain. I winced, my head snapped to the right, and then I saw her. No - I saw her! Party Peggy, and she did not wear a bra. How was such a thing merely possible?
I jumped into an upright position. I looked down at myself and I was shocked again. I was naked! Well, almost naked, I had the shoes on. I gasped in disbelief to myself: "I have done it with this fat woman" Then I bit into my clenched fist. I overcame it with an ice-cold shower of nastiness. I am out of energy, and I fell back on the mattress, I saw how a compost tub guested in Peggy´s tangled, curly hair. I looked at her, she is maybe thirty-five years old, her monstrous seems to be about ten pounds heavy, and what she whispered in my ear, I did not like at all!
"Well, my big one, you slept well?"

O God, I was inside this fat bitch.
DISGUSTING!
Her breath smelled like a distillery. Maybe mine
did not smell better, but at least I didn´t not build
my own distillery in a compost heap. I wanted to
get up but I could not. I gasped to myself while I
looked frozen at her and only after several
attempts, I succeeded to say following: "Go away"
She looked scared at me and said something like:
"What's wrong, sweetie? I am your Peggy. "
I was so angry: "Oh God!"
Then I turned my whole body to the left side of the
bed, and put my head over the bed edge and
began to choke. When I saw the bedroom floor, I
asked myself whether I am at my home. I looked
over the shoulder and saw Peggy. And how did
you come to my house? I had definitely drunk too
much at the New Year´s Eve night. I turned to
Peggy.
"Go away from my apartment!" I screamed so loud
so the mirror in the bedroom closed.
"What?" I saw someone hiding under the blanket
right from me, and is awake now. True. He even
spoke. "But - but why, what is this ...?"
My throat let out a cry of infernal rage. I did not
turn my head, I started to scream at the ceiling.
Saliva sprayed from my lips upward. 'Buckle' your
dishes on, you fat bitch, and get finally out of here!
"

She stared at me. I felt her staring, I could feel her
mental paralysis. I looked to the left. And took my

lamp and made her understand that I'm serious. I had been wondering about many things in my life, but one of the things about which I was surprised was undoubtedly the amazing fact how I could be with Peggy in such a short time. She left and I was finally alone in my bedroom. A moment later I heard someone knocking on the door of my apartment. I took the lamp.

I thought she came back. With a curse on my lips I shot up from the bed. It apparently did not help. It was always the same. It was not enough, to say anything, it was not enough to cry even. No, I have to ... I was curious to see what would it be this time. I went to the door and pulled the intercom button.

"What? " I hissed quietly in the plastic cracks.

A hesitation. Then her voice. "My Hand Bag! I could perhaps ..."

My Thumb slipped from the plastic knob. I went into the room back and saw the bag on the other side of the bed. Near the window. There it was. A cheap imitation of Louis Vuitton. I picked it up from the ground, then I opened the bedroom window.

I looked down.

Peggy was already coming from the doorway and shyly peered out upward. Somehow she had managed to get dressed. From there it looked like a brown wool wrap. In the middle of a cartwheel great, I saw her neck and stopped by sudden anticipation of what would come below the neck, I threw the bag to her.

I have missed the target for scarce two meters.

I just wanted to close my window again when I saw that her pocket abruptly stopped quite far from her when it hit the ground. Peggy's tits are bobbing in the direction of her pocket. Does this woman have an air bag too? They even floated in the air. Am I hallucinating? I opened the window for a while and leaned out. Someone took her handbag from the ground.

Someone? No. Not "someone".

FUCK, it was Rita!

I would prefer to sink in the ground right now because she saw me. Suddenly it was as if I looked in a mirror. I could imagine what a sight is it for: A disheveled, unshaven, with naked upper body guy throwing a bag from his window to a bar whore with XXXL-tits. Well done! She will never be my girlfriend after this. Shame on me!

Somewhere in my brain I heard the voice of some idiot wearing a Schell Hat: "Good friends stuck something like that away. And best ones as well." I gasped for breath, while I continued to stare at the road. This stupid voice in my head continues to talk: "Is not it like that, my friend? You would never land with her anyway, "accompanied by a bright, resounding jeers.

I closed the window. Scrubbed from the pitch, disgust and shame. That is what I feel. And only

after I had eaten a soup (fresh cooked), I came back
to myself. Then I went back to my bed again,
wandered the old bedding in the garbage. Then I
laid down and slept until the next morning.
When I woke up, I decided to spend the day in my
apartment.

In the afternoon my phone rang.
It was Rita.

"Well, did you sleep well?" she wanted to know.
At first, I was a little surprised. Otherwise, I
always answered with a rather scarce and
somehow slightly dry "Well, how are you?". She
lived two blocks away, and we met there or on a
"friendly sit-in" in our favorite pub - Bistro with
smoking lounge. Of course, only when none of us
were dating someone. "And, rested? " That was
something completely new.
"Yes, so far," I said and sat down on my big leather
couch in the living room. "I was celebrating
yesterday, at the birthday party of my work
colleague and it was pretty interesting."
I paused for a moment. Should I bring it up, or
rather not? Oh, what should it mean? "You came
up with the conclusion already, or"?
She did not say anything.
Then she changed the subject. "Would you like to
go on Saturday on a New Year's party with me? I
am invited, but I have no companion. And to be
constantly accosted by anyone, I do not want to. "

We are both quiet for a moment.

"So - what is your answer?" she impatiently digs deeper.

A beam of pure enthusiasm instantly brightened inner side of me. My pulse jumped up few bars, but I did not want to let her know that.

"Sure, done thing," I said while I tried to sound somewhat laconically. "Until now, I do not have any plans which applies totally great too! When do we meet?"

"Can I come to you at six? Then we can take a cub together. "

"Of course, but where?" I asked because I wanted to know where it is going to be.

"In the old factory," said Rita. I could listen to her anticipation. I knew the house. It offers space for at least two hundred people, and is equipped with the most modern disco-frills and excellent air-conditioning. "An old friend of mine has a birthday on New Year´s Eve. Cornelia - I think you've met her before. Of course, you need to bring anything like a present. So to speak, it is going to be a double party. She has rented the house for the evening, and there will definitely be quite a lot of guests. "

"I am happy," I said. After we had talked a little about trivialities and reaffirms the time of our meeting again, we both hung up.

Suddenly it was Friday night. My eyes fell on the digital digits of the DVD recorder. 17:59 pm. I

stood up and went to the door. Rita was one of the few women who were never late. She had perfect sense of time and could be precise even without the clock. I have never seen her late. And if she would be late I would ask her what happened, why she delayed, since she entrusted to me once, that being late shows disrespect to the person who is waiting. And she has never come too early as well. She was always on time, literally. It rings, I knew it should start ringing since my DVD Recorder displayed 18:00. I talked to her through intercom, pressed the button, with which I unlocked the door. Then I saw her through my door viewer. A habit of mine which I just could not take rid of it. And perhaps I did not want to make rid of it. Because I have always been a little paranoid. Already as a child. After I had seen that she isn´t in front of my door, I opened it but I heard Rita is coming by stairs. I noticed the clicking of the paragraphs on the stone floor of the staircase. She was walking slower and less smoothly than usual, because she did not apparently have her flat shoes which she prefer instead of few pumps otherwise.
I asked myself whether I was dressed appropriately. I wore a shirt with a white root pinstripe, the narrow, pleasant shaded long strips lined in a little lighter shade. Under my navy blue fabric trousers were elegant, dark brown shoes. To celebrate the day, I had on my gold watch as well. My jacket, a perfectly fitted two heron in bright

chest nut color, was elegant and sporty at the same time and could easily be worn with everything. And although I am sometimes not sure what I do and whether it is good enough, I thought I had an appropriate birthday gift for that occasion anyway. It was very nicely decorative and fancy packed bottle of Remy Martin - I saved this special one for special situation. Hopefully Rita liked it. With her I was never sure. She makes me confused. In the worst case, I was thinking whether I should leave the bottle at home? But what will be my present then. I do not have another one except it. She hated expensive gifts, because she was the one who thinks it is "waste of money". With herself but also with others. Which means that it should be taken for granted. For example she spent every year a fairly expensive holiday with one of her friends - and even if she was in a fixed relationship. Each time I got a post card. Usually, she flew to some luxury resorts with names that you do not really could keep in your head. She paid the price of a whole bottle for a single tiny umbrella drink. Supermarkets were outside of the hotel area, and in one of them the prices are two cents less than in the others. She did not want to buy there, even if she had only to wait ten minutes to cross the main road before green appears on the traffic lightening.

I heard she entered the last stair and could not fail to me inwardly a little arm. After all, we did not

see each other for more than four weeks, except the small interlude through my bedroom window.
The clicking of her paragraphs became louder and before I was aware of that, she stood already in front of me.

Rita was not among the women, who smiled very often, but this does not mean she was "strict" or even "weird". I would never say something like that about her. She was maybe a little cool. Something in her smile, easily recognizable came an equal and unpleased friendliness to an expression, and if she was happy about something, then her entire being was in that joy. Rita was full of ambition, but also of serenity. Her inner peace exuded focus above all because of her very special timbre of voice, the nature of innate pragmatism never lost its property reference pulse.
For me, she had always had an open ear and had a good advice when I needed it, and when I looked at her at that moment, I felt, even if only for a fraction of a second, the hot needle stitch of a perfidious fear that this could change.
She looked at me.
Rita was a classical beauty. Shoulder long red colored hair (actually, her natural hair color is stray dog blond) enriched her finely chopped, harmonic face. Her skin is gold colored instead brown and her almond eyes are so deep and if you walk in to immerse yourself, you will never find out again how to go out from there, and would

therefore like to stay forever. Her body was a perfect hard body. Hardly to find a gram of fat. Because she also worked hard. Particularly her breasts were perfectly portioned. Not too small and not too little. They would perfectly fit in my hand, I always thought. The same applies for her grand shaped butt. As set in stone. Just perfect!!!! If I dream about Rita or just think of her (and I do quite often), I always syringe and it is still so, within a few seconds.

And I could not remember she has ever looked so perfect like that night. A Type with Clamp Cap, somewhere in the background of my mind, was surprised to hear giggling.
And that is exactly what made me think for a while. If I had used my head before, then I would go in the bed with thick woman.
Rita had never perfume on herself, but today she did.
She smiled at me. It was a radiant smile, and I almost didn't notice that she said "Hello" to me. I saw her, but it came to me as if there is no image in my consciousness. I took all for granted, and at the same time I had the impression, but I was watching through it.
I heard my own voice like from a distance. It was a profound and long-drawn: "Hey you coupled with a broad smile. I asked you to come while I was a step aside in order to make you space."

Rita knew my tabernacle of many visits. She went after me and I shut the door behind her. In her right hand, she held a medium sized bag of artfully printed, thick paper. I followed Rita till the living room. In her lilac-colored net curtains, body forming costume from a smooth almost knee-length skirt and matching blazer, offered from the back with her perfectly shaped butt. It is a very pleasing sight. Her slim, straight legs had nylons, with a pattern of subtle snake lines.
Perfect outfit I would say. I liked it.
"Sit here ", I said to her. „What would you like to drink?"
"No, thanks. At the moment, nothing." Rita smiled at me and presented her carrying case. Then she sat down on a chair, after her blazer was stored. Among other things she wore was a ruffle cut blouse, not too dark with color-coordinated inlay discontinued and perfectly harmonized with her costume. Up on the pumps, which were once more a thorn for her. On her neck I recognized a thin antique silver chain, the fantasy form of a richly carved trailer made from the same material held in the middle of the dark plaid, sparkled ruby. I was not someone who notices jewelry but this time I did.
I sat down opposite her on the couch and looked deliberately quite intensively at her. She had an eyeshadow and even an eyeliner. Nothing was too much. Jus perfectly right. Everything underscored her natural beauty. Rita's lips shimmered in a

gentle, salmon-colored Pastellton, depending on the incidence of light.

She looked straight into my eyes. Rita has never turn her face while talking to someone, just because that person would find it rude and not nice from her.

Instead she would say or ask something to what commonly no one could answer neither she nor the opposite side. Marketing manager with high communication skills was actually what described her.

"I hope you did not buy anything." she friendly said - She sat upright in my chair and looked at me with subdued expectations.

"Never mind! " I said, without waiting for Rita's response. I was standing at the narrow side chest of drawers made of polished walnut. Behind my couch position, I had left my gift. Now I took it from there and showed her the bottle with the noble drops showed on the cellophane film, which was stamped by colorful ruffled tapes. I put it on the glass plate of the flat table between us. Rita saw it first and then took it into hands to see the bottle and the details on it better and then she put it back where it was before.

"And what do you mean? „I asked her.

"Nice, "she said and looked again at the bottle for a few seconds as if she wanted to rest for a while and to think about something. My Cognac had just given the green light. I smiled spontaneously.

Rita had brought her friend artistically forged plate in the form of a sun. She carefully pulled it out from the paper bag, where she put it. The entire plate was covered with gold leaf, and in its middle, from small stones was formed "20". "The number represents age of my friend, actually our friend because we both know her for such a long time", commented Rita, while I am fascinated about the gift. I stretched out my arms and she gave me the plate so that I could take a closer look." A wonderful gift", I nodded affirmative. "Something very special." a compliment to Rita's appearance was on my lips, but I hesitated. It was not one of the women who wanted to hear compliments on how good she looks. I instinctively know it. Our long lasting friendship made me think like that. Rita preferred to be recognized for something she did. Wonderful look was not something she wanted to show. "Your friend will be very happy, "I said and gave her the plate back. She thanked me with a warm smile and stowed it back safely in her bag.

"I have not presented you Cornelia? "She asked again.
"I cannot remember anyone called Cornelia, maybe when I see her I will know who she is."
"We have to go then now", she said. "Can you call a taxi for us?"
"Of course", I replied immediately and took my cell phone, which had been on the table, next to the

drinks. I knew Rita long enough to know that "we" is usually lacking. While I was searching for the taxi number, she bent a little forward and smiled subtle. Her view was a bit curious and at the same time happy.

I ordered the taxi.

When we arrived at the old factory, I wanted to pay the fare, but Rita insisted to share it. I opened the door and took her bag so that she could easily get out of the car. We entered the local together. Cornelia noisy welcomed Rita she always had uninhibited joy to see her. They exchanged Wang kisses, and Rita congratulated her for her birthday. I was thinking when I saw Cornelia last time. But no, I couldn´t remember. That was long ago since I saw her for the last time. After Cornelia got the ornate dish from Rita, she was over the moon. In the background of the huge, semi-dark room, I could see colorful lightened garden, where the party was just to start. The music was loud enough, and nobody wanted to stop it. Everything was decorated with garlands and air snakes on the thick oak parquet. Glittering stars and confetti were also distributed all over the place. The buffet was open but no one has touched it yet. Shells with punch alternated with cold plates, the meat dishes and seafood were prepared and served as well. There were colorful Berlin, fried pastry and other things which were generated in abundance. The wood-paneled cooling boxes waited for sparkling wine and champagne. At the short end of the hall

there was a precious illuminated bar with a
cocktail specialist. Everyone was there. I took the
beautiful fragrance of fresh mint and got
immediately appetite for a Mojito, my favorite
cocktail. Rita stood a small step aside and looked
at me. I congratulated Cornelia and gave her my
gift. She was surprised and said to me with a loud
and very warm voice: "Thank you". Then she
asked us if we want to drop. Discrete staff in white
shirts with black fly, suit trousers and waistcoat
observed us in the event. Ten of them were
distributed in the background of the room to make
sure Cornelia's guests are enjoying the party.
We met a lot of new guests later on. Cornelia
welcomed all with the same dedication, but not so
intimate as she welcomed Rita. We were standing
behind the buffet and then went to one of the hall
distributed standing tables. In our glasses was
sparkling wine. Our bottle was half empty and we
left it on the table next to us. I want to take her
hand first, but I did not do it since Rita was not
drinking that much. Only two glasses. Perhaps
even a third around midnight. I tried to put the
alcohol in her glass so that it looks like the liquid
she previously had in it. When I looked at the
marks rested in the Cabinets, I found that this idea
is perhaps not entirely great.
Rita's concern about possible, unwanted speech
proved to be unfounded. But only as long as her
companions were safe and not caught. In the
meantime, Cornelia tried to interrupt us again and

again and particularly to dedicate my girlfriend,
but always careful so that she is not neglecting
other guests. Pairs danced occasionally to the fleets
of music on the dance floor where the music was
louder. My girlfriend praised the food in detail
and expressed the fear that it could be too much
for her.
 "In the new year, we will slim down everything „I
said relaxed. "Alcohol also burns the fat."
"Do you think so?" she looked at me a little unsure.
I have to convince her to drink a little more. She
didn´t relate it to the food, but to herself. Although
she had a dream figure, she always thought she is
too thick.
"And even though you are best friends who can
say everything to each other, you can´t still tell
her", said the leprechaun from somewhere in my
head.
I departed your question. "Come and let us see
what the bar has to offer„ I said. "I bet they have
also mojito, and it is not possible to get it decently
mixed almost anywhere. I want to know what the
man who mixes the drinks can do."
When I wanted to go to him, Rita put her hand on
my forearm.
"Wait", she said and drank quickly the small drink
sparkling wine that was still in the glass and
followed me then to the bar.
Two couples were already there, one of them
closely rolled, the other with a little distance, but
looking at each other. All of them were about our

age. Rita and I sat at one of the two comfortable leather curved stool, a bit away from the others. Anyone who wanted to, could be in the small lounge. The bar was upstream.
Like always, I ordered a Mojito, after Rita, who ordered first mineral water. She got it with ice cubes, strawberry and one lemon slice on the edge of the glass. After I said my order, he mixed the fruity exotic aroma of lime in a large tumbler glass with the spicy scent of fresh mint. The brown cane sugar was so finely crushed that I did not have any crystal on the tongue when I tasted the straw. It stuck between the lips and the noble rum connected its mild aroma in perfect harmony with the other ingredients. I had to close my eyes and could not stop drinking. I was drinking without even taking a breath and continued doing so until my glass was finally empty. I had my eyes still closed. Even after it. I could taste it still on my lips. Only during the subsequent breath I opened my eyes again - and looked directly at Rita.
"My best Mojito, favorite drink for a long time", I left them smiling.
She sipped at her water, but she could still see me. The bartender returned and asked friendly, whether I still want something. I ordered the same again and took three glasses respectively. I was quite hard drinking and had already drunk five glasses of alcohol. However I was in a female companion that evening and not with friends because I did not want to bring Rita in a silly

situation, even if I was there at the birthday party of her friend.

I took my next glass. Rita looked over my glass and smiled. I took her hand and held it with the straw on her side.

"A small drink you must absolutely try, "I said. Rita smiled as if she was waiting for a little courage which will make her do that. The she put her hand a little forward where the drinks were standing. But she was still unsure whether she should do it. I was looking forward to the result.

"Really tasty, "I friendly said to her.

Cornelia appeared from nowhere. We were standing close to each other with the hands on shoulders. We could not deny a conscience. I was sure she knew about Rita and me, how good and close friends we are. But at the same time I wondered what she actually thinks about it.

Rita wanted to go to toilet shortly, and I took the opportunity to take my second drink. I went to the lounge and sat in one of the cozy armchairs. As Rita returned, she went to leave her blazer. She came to me, and stayed.

"Let us dance", she said and stretched out her hand against me.

I thought: *Shit,* I cannot move myself even for a meter and I do not know how to dance. So what should I do now? To tell her that I do not dance in the public? Or if she can just forget it? I did not say anything, only grinned and took her hand at the same time. The not-to-be-fast beat of the music required sophisticated way of dancing. Some of those who were already on the dance floor moved imperceptibly, some had still a champagne glass in hand, other danced closely rolled. Rita moved completely natural to the beat of the music, as if she had never done anything else. She put her hand on my shoulder, and I had no problems to follow her rhythm. When the music was a little bit faster, she let me go and turned back again in front of me and did so in the circuit. During a rotation, she stopped and turned her back to me and continued dancing. The thumb and index finger of her hands followed the beat of the music in the height of her head. I came very close to Rita, and as she rotated, I put my hands gently on her hips. She put her hands on my shoulders, moving it further and watched me direct in the eyes. Without a smile. Her hands moved slowly deeper, over my upper arms, and then she slowly approached me. But not completely. We have never looked to each other so directly without saying anything. We have never been so close like at this moment. And I have never had my hands where I had that time. I usually put my hands on her waist. But now they remained there. The music, which was pretty quiet, did not make me angry even if it did before. I could not believe how I change my mind about everything when it comes to Rita. My eyes were wide open but I saw nothing more except her. I was not able to see perfectly since I lost my consciousness and I obviously needed a rest in

order to be able to perceive what is actually going on there. Our movements were a standstill at the same time. My hands went slowly down. And when my eyes were closed before our lips touched, I felt so great as if the time stopped and everything became unimportant.
That perfect moment.
Perfect unity.
Absolute fusion.
Meaning a resolution of all opposites.
At least one of them.
Produced in the offense.
Heaven and earth merged with one another, and I every fear of dying has gone, just for those few seconds of my life.

It was the only thing that was worth waiting for.

And so it happened.
Although I have never quite understood. I was the best friend to her.
Rita and I were together for the New Year's Eve party, but we left it together as well.
I have never loved someone like Rita. I am admitting. Even if there were a lot of them in my life.

Other women were only women. Except Rita. They came and went. No one did not mean anything to me. They were only apparently there. I hid myself with them before my obsession of Rita. They were good enough to

But although we have always mutually protested
our love, remained to me over and over again,
even if only very gentle sting of a doubt, not
spared, deep seated somewhere in my soul and
sometimes silent, yet unmistakable, poses the
question whether I just might be her another
"temporary partner". We were already a few
months together, but we still lived in separate
apartments. However we stayed almost always
together in one of the two. In the last summer we
went on an excursion to a beautiful lake. I
Made the proposal to go in one of the restaurants
on the river bank, but Rita wanted to walk around
the lake rather. So we started. Next to the lake
grew a long-drawn hill in quite a considerable
height. Even as a little boy I loved wooded hills
and I do still. So, I proposed her hill climbing.

When I was six or seven years old, my mother
dragged me there. It was the only trip she has ever
taken with me. I bristled at the first time because I
preferred to watch television (My step mother, has
never let me alone to do what I want), but when
my mother said that she met my father there,
nothing could stop me anymore. And it took me
years to come back to this very special place for
me. I repeatedly made alone (Rita was the first and

only one I ever took there) trips to the top of the hill. It was the only place I knew where my father was once, and I secretly expected deep in myself to meet him there. My father, whom I did not met, is still loved and missed. But he was never there.

Rita did not want to do it at first, but I persuaded her. Maybe I wanted to assure myself only,
that my father is not up there, waiting for me. Or he had left a message for me, or a small hint that only I could understand. Maybe I only wanted to know that there is no one I knew. And no one I loved.
Rita was beside me.
The road ran in serpentine, but I still knew old abbreviations. When we finally left it at one point again and the next Serpentine of
could see actual path disappearing behind a bend, Rita seemed all
Orientation to have lost. She breathed audibly, but would have due to their sportiness
they cannot even be in the neck of breath.
She asked me to stop for a moment. She looked unsure around.
"Is there now upwards or downwards again?" She asked, pointing to the spot behind the Serpentine eluded our eyes.
"I think down," I told her. I was not at the moment even quite sure, and the course of the path left nothing in this direction to see.

So I went on the visible end to approximately one hundred meters away, to convince me. I told Rita "I´ll be e right back", because I thought she would perhaps have to recover for a moment. But when I made only few steps forward, I heard what she told me, with a slight, almost imperceptible tinge - it was panic? -in the voice calling after: "You are letting me to stand here and breathe, or"?
I stood thunderstruck, first unable to understand the full meaning of her question; incapable to understand it.
"What?"
Even as I uttered that one word in disbelief, I turned on the spot
around. I hesitated a moment, then I went up to her. I spread my arms out slightly.
"Rita."
I heard my own voice, as she choked with concern outright. I took Rita in my arms and held her for several minutes. I felt that it seemed to take an eternity before she put her arms around me. When I gently pulled away from her, she did not look at me, she looked past me.
"I think we should go back down over there," she said and stayed trying to focus her sight on the path.
"Are you okay?" I asked.
"Yes, all right," she said - almost a little repellent as I believed at the time.
I took her hand. "Let us look," I said to her, and we walked together to the path that actually led us

further down. So I asked Rita if she would rather
go back to the lake, but she accompanied me to the
summit, after she had previously checked whether
it is too far.
On the way back I avoided further abbreviations.
At the top there was a ten-meter tower. Steel steps
led up to a viewing platform. Besides us, there was
no one present. I did not mind higher altitudes,
and Rita wanted to go up necessarily, and so
entered
we finally the platform.
"The view is totally super," Rita said with
unexpected enthusiasm.
"Yes," I answered, "I was as a boy here more often."
She took my hand, and together we finally stood
before the reassuring high
we enjoyed a while the view on that radiant
summer day. And I wondered if my parents stood
so back then. In love? Have they ever been in this
tower? My mother told me then just that they have
met here at the summit, but not exactly where.
And what they were doing here. Perhaps you were
even conceived here? I heard from somewhere a
voice in my head.
Rita held her right hand as a shield over her eyes
and looked at an airplane that moved at a greater
distance with his silver silhouette over the blue
sky.
I had to remember that the time to fly together is
coming soon, along with my best friend Rita. I put
my hand down and Rita completely turned to me.

After a few seconds she did the same. She stood in front of me and looked into my eyes.

"Rita," I began cautiously and my left hand was her right before I then spoke. "Would you - I mean - are we in this summer flying together? Just you and me, and nobody else? Two or maybe three weeks, the two of us alone - no stress, no worries, nothing but sun, sand and water, and a few nice cocktails at sunset. What do you think?"

She saw me on to, and something unexplainable stole her sight into clear blue gaze. "Where?" She asked softly and curious at the same time.

I knew she loved the sea and rummaged in my memory feverishly for any popular destination. "What do you think of Madeira, in Portugal?" I said.

She suddenly covered my neck and gave me a kiss on the lips. "All right," she said and held me for a while so firmly.

I looked into her eyes.

I wanted to tell her: "I love you", but something held me spontaneously against it. At first I did not know what it was, but then I realized it. It was fear! I told her a hundred times that I love her, but now I was afraid to say it, because I was sure that she was afraid as well at the moment. No! "Wonderful" when I had "super! " I did not propose her the purpose of our trip, I understated "alright".

Just one kiss on my lips.

A kiss, and not "I love you"

This left my inner alarm bells ring. The gentle sting of doubt in me turned very quickly into "fear". The fear that she would leave me. A kiss alone is no longer enough for me. I needed the confirmation in the form of the words "I love you", which came from her mouth. But they did not come out. I was confused (as often happened in our relationship). When we went back to the lake, I was subsequently somehow glad that she had not satisfied on the platform above that I hopefully did not intend to bring them down to happen from there. I quickly let these thoughts fall silent again. I loved her. All I needed is to know whether she loves me too.

And yet I suddenly fell upon a nagging question, like a predator - just before we reached the lake again. I did not miss anything on the hilltop? Was there something that I had completely forgotten and would want to see?

Perhaps he was there. Maybe he has stood in the corner, which I had not looked at.

To the lurked corner, from which Rita had distracted because she him perhaps, but did not want to tell me.

I turned around and found myself again up the hill. Up, up to the viewing platform, such as a steel memorial above all towered.

And I saw it!

A figure! A blurred figure with the body of a man, and he was in the full sun light just before

The tower. Your father? I heard again from somewhere out of my head the voice. I let Rita's hand hastily to shield my eyes. But there was nothing more. Even as I raised my right hand to the eyes, the shape disintegrated and was no longer visible.

"What is it?" Asked Rita, and in her voice a little concern with.

I moved my hand back down and grabbed her. "Nothing, Rita," I said smiling at her. "I just wanted to see the ancient hills again."

And then we went to the lakeside restaurant, which we had almost reached.

I held Rita's hand, and suddenly I felt light and free. So as I was enveloped in a perfect aura of absolute, pure happiness. No one had been there, I had yet to see exactly.

No one I knew. And no one I loved.

Eventually I told Rita that I would like to live with her. Which they thought rushed. Not that she doubted our relationship, as she assured me she was just think that we should let go slow. The real reason for their refusal was that she was very attached to her small two-room apartment, and space for two people offered not easy. Although she never said it, I knew it was true, everything else showed in my eyes no sense. And therefore I could not be angry.

The theme, with their apartment, then never came back to language. I did not dare to ask to not catch me a rejection, I also felt that it was now his turn to raise this issue again. But nothing came. We never talked about it again.

By the time I noticed that she always distanced myself was over, and I initially thought that it was normal. As in any long leading relationship was so common just. But the whole thing had something strange. I often caught her as she watched me, and usually with an incredulous expression. As if she had seen a ghost. Even when we sat together on the couch and we saw a movie.

And four months ago has finally happened what I had almost expected: She ended the relationship. But the reason they called me is a mystery to me to this day.

The night that she left me started promising. Since I secretly felt that it was not particularly well ran with us, and I no longer have the words "I love you" of you heard for a long time, which at the same time meant to me that I did not have any confirmation, which made me almost crazy decided I bring you a nice romantic and even cooked dinner in my apartment. However, it was not just a dinner, but a four course meal. As an appetizer there was a Mandarinencobbler and as a starter I served a vegetable salad with shrimp and toast triangles. The second course consisted of a salmon-shrimp soup with cream and fresh herbs. The third gear, the crowning main course, a delicate butterfly steak with flavored chive mustard butter, croquettes. The pivoted apple corners with pistachio and even whipped cream, made dessert. The champagne we drank this was a Billecart-Salmon Brut rosé. In my CD player the HIM Best-of Album ran at a comfortable level. The right music for the bedroom was already prepared Goodnight Moon Shivaree in a loop.

Rita was initially somewhat restrained when I presented her food and beautifully set table. Initially a word was hardly spoken, and Rita thawed only really toward the end of the second gear on. We came off the branch on the floor and talking about this and that. Just like in the old days, even though I was the great entertainers, managed Rita, always follow suit me, and so I spoke places in one evening more than in a whole year. We changed after we had finished eating, the dining table to the couch and made ourselves comfortable there. We snuggled even after a long time again.

And then in a particularly intimate moment, I told her that I loved her always, from the moment of our getting to know each other, on the playground. And that I have never trusted myself all these years, to confess her. And that we would probably never have come together if she had not taken the initiative. If I'd had even the slightest idea that this confession, which was very romantic and above all honest in my eyes, made sure that she left me, I would never have said it.

She was not touched by this confession, as I have

presented to her. She was outraged over indignant, she was furious. She accused me of miserable liar.
I am a liar.
Although I still tell the truth, to illustrate her as my great love for her, I was accused of being a liar.
I understood nothing.
Rita said, I would have you know, when we first met from day one us to lie to my love, because I never told her. You could with my cowardice not live and I had never been basically anything other than a miserable, pathetic coward.
And before I knew it, it was out.
Forever.
Attempts to save our relationship were unsuccessful. I thought that it would be best thing if I initially accepted her request and was waiting only once. And if I leave her in peace - until she had calmed down and remembered that all not so bad - she might yet come to the realization. That she begins to miss me. I was hoping for a debate. But none of this came out. She did not tell a single word to me.

Anyway, I did not mourn the past time because I'm still sitting on the motorway service area and will be probably accused for double murder. Because of Ben, this strange voice in my phone! So I'm trying to concentrate myself now.
When Rita would like to help me, I would have to return to Mainz. And I still do not know how to get away from here. With my car I cannot go on, I

do not have enough money for gasoline and it is simply too dangerous when they are investigating after me.

The only way that I do have here, is to travel on as a hitchhiker. I have to make just a good story of how I got here. I should not mention my and that I had an accident because they would ask me why I did not call the breakdown service. Also, I may have to find someone who moves in my direction. But first I'm going to eat something. I climb out of my car and walk to the Burger King branch, which is located here at the motel. I am reluctant, to put myself literally on a platter, but what to do. I'm hungry and the food is pretty damn good.

At the entrance I meet with a guy who seems familiar to me.

"Hey, do I know you?" I asked him after I apologize for my carelessness.

"I do not know," he replies and dry eyes suspiciously.

"I am sure I have met you," I say in a conciliatory tone. "What is your name?"

"Paul." My counterpart acts somewhat reluctantly

"I am Dirk, we know each other."

There is a break for a moment.

"Sorry, I do not know anyone named Dirk", he says and runs hastily away.

"You know Frank? " I said looking him leaving.

"Oh my God", he moans annoyed, and continues walking but falls down from his pocket.

"Hey, did you lose something", I scream after him, but he is not responding.

From here, where I am, I do not know what it is, and before Paul disappears, I run out quickly to pick it up. It is a black Android phone. I pick it up and call Paul. But I no longer see him, and no car can be seen or heard, which is started and drives away. I run over the whole place, looking after him, without success. As if he was swallowed by the earth.

I finally give up and go to my ultimate goal of getting food.

Immediately after I enter the Burger King, I stop for a moment, and look around. I take eye contact with the guests. I start to sweat and get nervous. If you are really paranoid on it, you think, all talk about you. Actually for me it is a normal state. But now it's something else, because I'm on the run. As they stare at me all and whispering (Or am I the only one?) I do not understand what they say, but it is certainly not nice. (Look, there is the killer being searched). I do not understand what they say, but nice, it is not intended. (Here look, there is the killer, is wanted after). It seems to me that the food gets stuck in their throat when they saw me. I try to stay cool. And just go quickly (and totally stiff, as if I had a stick in the ass, SUPER AUFFÄLIG) to the bar. The employees of the fast food store who are here treated as immigrants, seem to be ignoring me which somewhat soothed me in my paranoid delusions.

After I took small menu, I look at the Android phone for more details about Paul, who I believed to know. The contact list is practically empty. Not even ten entries are saved. Numbers of the breakdown assistance, the emergency call, his mother and sister were also dubbed as well. In addition, by a certain Marko, Steven, Tim, Kevin and Karl-Heinz. Of the latter I find a stored SMS, which is the only thing at the same time.

It says: *You are very attractive and smart. I want to make love with your brain. Atergo. But I have to get it first out of your head.*

In addition, I find an email from the sender SuperTyp@hot-mail.com: shit into my mouth and call me Supertyp ... You cunt!

It seems to me that the word "cunt" with "V" was written.

I ask, first the other guests of the restaurant, if they go in the direction of Mainz, and if they could take me with them. Unsuccessful trial. So I clatter all from standing in the parking lot, and newly added. And after nearly two hours I finally got lucky. A man who introduces himself as Helmut Berger, and is on the road to Kaiserslautern, offers me to take a detour and thereby insert a stopover in Mainz. He is in his late forties, a head shorter than I, and has a bit overweight, stubble and thick horn-rimmed glasses on his nose. His slightly wavy hair is a mix of gray and black. He drives an old Mercedes Kombi, which conveys a checkbook neat impression. I introduce myself as Robert Weißmüller, a hitchhiker who wants to travel all over Germany. I explain to him that I am in an emergency situation, because my previous portability along with my luggage, where also my wallet was, has been just stolen. In Mainz, my alleged aunt would be waiting for me which will help me get out of trouble.

"Please get in and feel yourself like at home. I will help if I can, "he says to me in a cheerful chatty. I sit at the passenger seat and put on the belt. It seems that his old Mercedes makes a very neat impression from the inside; except for some dust on the fitting and the overflowing ashtray, everything looks very neat. On the shelf in front of me are numerous pens, with a cheap plastic cladding, which are all printed with the same logo that is similar to a light bulb. Below spot are four pencils that are unusual long and thick. All of them fully filled out. On those stays XXXL ... and something else as well. I cannot see more from here. After we left, I notice a recurring clatter of metal that seems to come out of the trunk.

"That's the metal cladding of my lamps," he tells me.

»Lamp?"

"Yes, I am trade representatives who gets rid of LED lighting to industry and municipalities."

"There are now LED lighting?" I ask skeptically.

"Oh, yes, as a replacement for almost all lamps that exist in the world."

"So, you mean just flashlights, spotlights or headlights of cars - what we all know"?

"No, everything is already old; there are now LED bulbs, tubes to replace fluorescent lamps, outdoor lamps, and HQL or street lights."

He takes out a business card from his pocket and hands it to me. I look at it for a while, and then say: "Interesting, and how it goes"?

"Very good indeed," he says, looking at me with big shining eyes. He pointed to the pile of pens, and then says. "Just look, there are pencils of my biggest customers"

I take one of these really powerful pencils, and read what it says: XXXL - FURNITURE GIANT

"I know them, but you make advertising with these German basketball players, right?" I ask and touch with my index finger the extremely sharpened and quite thick Minne and prick so nearly to the skin of my finger.

"That's right, they recently became the market leader in Germany and is currently building numerous production facilities throughout Europe."

"Okay," I say somewhat perplexed.

"And now I got the order, all existing buildings with my LED lighting to retool and the new ones should have the same light resources." He makes a short break. "I will make the order for their daughter company *"pointed Mintz"* this is the toothpick with the taste of mint".

"Yes, I know ... wow, I impressed.

"You know, you save with this new lamp
replacement a lot of energy ", he says.
"Oh, yes?"
"Between seventy and ninety percent of the
electricity costs are reduced, and in addition is
added up to ten times longer." He lights a cigarette
and offers me one. I answer with thanks and say:
"It's all madness, I would not have thought."
"Most of them do not, because the subject is
unfortunately not yet paid, there is too little
attention in the media. In addition, large power
companies try to avoid this as much as possible,
because it is bad for business. "
"I can imagine," I say, and I realize that this is the
first normal conversation that I lead for almost two
days. The subject interested me, although not at
all, but at least he is not a crazed psychopath who
wants to attach me something - for example, two
murders.
He talks for a while about his business, and he is
quite for a moment. What I find very pleasant,
because our LED topic is a bit annoying. The dusk
is already well advanced, and while Helmut
Berger turns on the headlights of his Mercedes, he
asks me where I'm coming from and what I'm
doing so, except hitchhiked to drive across
Germany.
"I come from the north and have recently studied
psychology, and now I have the degree in my
pocket" I make a break, I lie to him.
"And why are you than hitching rides?"

"Oh, I wanted to do it from time to time ... a small dream of my childhood. Free and unbound by Germany ... and perhaps explore other parts of Europe. Let's see where it impels me, "I lie on and I'm doing pretty stalled. What I am actually talking about?

"Yes, you can say that again," I say, and have to think of the woman's body that I buried in the woods and had apparently fucked.

"But you do not seem as if you come from the north," he notes. "You sound like someone who comes from Hessen or Rheinland-Pfalz."

"Yes ... that is because I have lived some time with my aunt in Mainz. Since then, I probably got some of this Rheinhessen dialect. "

"Have you studied there?"

"No, no, I have studied elsewhere." Shit, I cannot think of any other university.

"I guess that you do not have any woman or children?"

"No, I do not," I say and I am glad that he does not ask which university I have studied at. Then he says: "I am already married for almost thirty years, but children have not been given to my wife and me."

I do not want to know why, and I hope that he finally keeps his stupid mouth closed. And he actually did.

"And your parents, what do they do?" He completely unexpectedly asks me.

"My father, I have never met him, and my mother, she died from a cancer." The words come like a shot out of my mouth, and I am pretty annoyed. Moreover, for a change, I am saying the truth. He has struck dumb.

I believe that I hate Mr. Berger. I think I even hate many people. I think I always have something misanthropic in me and I wonder where that all came from? While Mr. Berger might be very nice and very helpful, without him I would most likely be in this shit even longer, but I believe that I still hate him.

I impatiently look at the digital clock in his car. Meanwhile, it is already dark outside.
"We would be there soon, right?" I ask back.
"I guess after three quarters of an hour."
When he just wanted to ask me one of his stupid questions, the ring from the Android phone that I have in my pocket, brings Mr. Berger abruptly to silence. He sets out in a face, as if he was struck by lightning. I apologize halfheartedly for interrupting his speech and take up the call of the unknown subscriber. I am ashamed a little before answering the call, because this call cannot be meant for me, but since Mr. Berger holds its flap at least for a brief moment, I feel all right.
"Hello?"
"Hello Dirk, how are you?"
It's the voice!

But how is that possible?
"Where did you get the number?" I ask shocked.
"You can guess three times."
"Do you know this Paul, or what?"
"That does not matter now. What is important at the moment for you, is that I know Mr. Berger. "
"What?" I ask confused.
I do not understand anything.
"You heard correctly, and he knows who you are."
"I don´t believe a word you say."
"Believe what you want, but you're knotless tapped us into a trap," he says with spiteful satisfaction.
My mind races. My heartbeat is accelerating. What a sick game is running here? "What do you want from me?" I am upset inwardly, but before I ask this question, I force myself to calm down.
»Give you a chance to keep the game going further."
"What do you mean?" I notice from the corner of his eye that Berger looks at me.
"Maybe I've told Mr. Berger to take you directly to the police. Then it's over for you. Or you take now this chance that I give you, to try to get rid of this stupid guy, then we play a little further, and perhaps you win at the end? "
"You're trying to put me into a trouble again" I say, trying to speak as quietly as possible, so that Berger cannot clearly understand it.
"It would be better for you, if you kill him."
"I should kill you!"

I look over at Berger, who stays completely shocked after my last statement on the phone. The only thing he does is taking another cigarette. Our eyes meet briefly when he ignites. In his eyes is something uncanny, as he would like to tell me following: "Yes, I know all about it, you have tapped us into the trap."

The voice speaks again: "Yes, suicide would be the best solution in your case, but so far we have not been yet. That's why Mr. Berger must now believe in it. "

"I will not kill that man!" I say softly, but in a determined tone.

"Come on, Carry it easy. Secretly, you want it too, otherwise we would not be talking to each other."

"You sick bastard!" I hurl at him with contempt.

"People who live in glass houses should not throw stones. Now turn yourself around "

"No!" I say it so loudly so that my passenger hears it for sure.

"Suit yourself, I've just offered you. I wish you then a lot of fun in a small cell in which you will land, and indeed for the rest of your life. "

The voice hangs up. I am confused and do not know what to think now.

Then Berger asks: "Are you all right?"

"Yes ... everything is okay," I say with an open mouth, without looking at him.

I am troubled terribly when his cell phone starts ringing. I almost jumped up from the seat.

Through my behavior, Mr. Berger also scared and

then says: "Just calm down my boy, this is going to
be my wife."
He starts the conversation with the words *Hello
you*. I am so tense that I cannot move. I wonder if
someone would so welcome his wife on the phone.
"Yes, I have it," is the next thing he says.
I'm suspicious.
Who does he mean? About me? Has the voice of
Ben but told the truth? "Everything is going
according to the plan, do not worry, we will be
there on time. Did I just the word "we" part and
"Everything is going according to the plan"?
The Android phone vibrate briefly. An SMS, is the
fact: "Did you hear, Dirk? It all goes to the plan ;) "
The panic comes over me.
"Who's there on the phone" I ask it loudly.
"Shah ..." is all I get as a response.
"Who's there on the phone?" I ask again
emphatically.
He dismisses only and gives me so to understand
that he will give me some time. But I cannot
restrain myself easily.
"Tell me with whom you are speaking there!" I
commend him. Distrust has degenerated into pure
paranoia. Who's there on the phone? His wife or
the voice? I need to know, and that now!
But I get no answer, so I asked him again: "Who
are you talking about"
He holds the phone away and looks at me as he
says: "It is upon request, but you should take a rest
first"!

I look at him straight in the eyes, and there I can see again: Yes, I know all about you, you have tapped us into the trap.

I can literally read him from his eyes, and I now know. He speaks with the voice. They are in cahoots, and they want to take me back to the track.

He turns away from me and holds his cell phone to his ear: "So, here I am again," he says, and then "No, he does not make any problems, everything is under control."

I reach the pile of pens, lying on the counter in front of me, and take one of those big pencils and pursue it with full force in his neck. I catch him in front, below his larynx. He cries out, and his eyes are wide open. He drops the phone and grabs my head. He pushes so hard, as if he wants to crush himself and looks directly at me. His eyes are rigidly staring and in his incredulous look can be clearly seen a mixture of despair and fear of death. He stools his eyes briefly in pain together, his mouth is half open and he chokes, grabs it by Run, blood begins to run out of his mouth. The Mercedes begins to lurch, I reach the steering wheel. His firm grip on my head loosens, it becomes weaker, and there is still blood coming out of his mouth. He is still trying to gasp for air, and trying with his free hand to grasp the pencil to pull out of his neck but he did not succeed. I make it, his foot moves down from the accelerator step and we lose the control over the car. I let him roll on my shoulder.

I am completely out of breath and watching how the man tries to grasp air and gurgles blood but shortly after that he dies on the driving seat. It fortunately happens very quickly. The blood runs from the pricked neck and drips into clothing.

I start violently to ventilate the car and have the feeling that I am going to faint at the moment. But I'm too angrily grabbing his phone and yelling into it: "You, asshole, have probably never thought that I would really do it, or"?

I held my breath, my upper body bobbed frantically back and forth, while I sweated, the phone pressed so hard my ears that the blood stopped to circulate. Just as the blood of the one who crouched on the seat next to me. The person who no longer stirred. The person, I have just killed!

"Hello? Who's there? What have you done with my husband? "

Fear came over me. It is as if the fear in that voice came to me and put completely under its control. The fear in this unknown voice.

In this woman's voice.

O my God, what have I done?

Everything is spinning in my head. I killed a man who was trying to help me. I made his wife a widow and she had to listen to everything. He has finally managed. He has led me to take a human life without no reason.

I am shocked and disgusted from myself.

I open the passenger door in panic and jump out. I throw Berger´s phone towards guardrail where it disappears into the behind-growing bushes.
I want to run away, but I do not know where. I'm on the stupid highway. I need the Mercedes. I have to get Berger´s corpse out of here.
I run to the driver's side and open the door, I have to hurry before someone passes by and sees us. Fortunately there is very little traffic today, which is strange, we are after all in a fucking highway, where are others actually? Not that I would need somebody in this moment, but it is already very strange. But whom am I talking to about something that does not exist? Berger is very heavy, I need all my strength to heave him out of the car and make sure not that he does not defile me with blood. I do not think about the DNA evidence, which I characterized bequeath to Berger at this moment. I took him to the crash barrier, lift him with my very last strength and let it fall down. His body rolled down over the slope and disappeared into the dense green.
Before going back into the Mercedes, I look briefly at the driver's seat, which has gotten as clear as no blood touched it. But actually there is one little drop, I wipe it away with a handkerchief, sit down and start driving the car.

I am still in shock, everything seems so unreal.
A sudden onset of noise scared me to death.
It is the Android phone. Damn, that's still there!

The display shows the number of Dennis. I am afraid. I push off the call and throw the Android phone into the footwall of the passenger seat.

I imagine that the voice is speaking to me over the loudspeakers in Mercedes:

Do you really believe that you love to me will go so easily?

Searching Help II

And now here I am.

I am still at the same place. With my back to Rita's door while I was telling her my horror trip of the last hours. In the hope that she will believe me. That she could muster a kind of pity for me, so that she can feel an inner urge which will tell her to help me.
One thing is clear, all alone, I cannot get out of this

thing.

"And what happened after that?" She asks me.

"How, what happened after that?" I ask back.

"Well, how are you now here?"

True, there was something else indeed. How did I get here? The last thing I remember, as I have imagined, after the murder of Berger, is listening to the voice on the speaker in the car. And then I am suddenly standing here in front of her apartment. What happened in between and where is the car? I cannot remember that I have parked the car in front of the building, let it alone to come here and Rita. I rummage through my pockets for the car keys. But there is nothing, there is not even a trace of the Android phone. My pockets are completely empty.

"Honestly, I do not know what actually happened," I say to her, and then: "I must have blacked out, that is the reason why I really cannot tell you. «

Unfortunately.

Since my story is incomplete, there is no credibility in her eyes. She does not know every detail. For this last part I remain guilty, because I do not know more about it, which means that something is missing: My memory. But perhaps I cannot deliberately remember everything? Maybe something so terrible in these dark hours has happened that I have buried any reminder deep inside me - because I could not bear to be aware of that? She interrupts the flow of thoughts in my

head by saying to me: "That's a pretty hair-raising story which you have served me here."
"Yes, I know, but it's the truth."
"So, if all this really should be the truth, then ..."
She does not dare to speak further.
"Then?"
"Then I cannot believe that you have actually driven with a corpse!" The horror and disgust can be clearly heard in her voice.
"Yes ... I cannot," I say, look here to the ground. The shame is probably written literally on my face, and I try to hide it. Now I'm really glad that the door is locked and that she cannot see it. However, I am a bit pissed off about her statement. I finally killed a man, and she showed no reaction at all and suspected me of having murdered my best friend. But all this seems to be merely incidental in her eyes, because I had had a sex with a dead woman. However, that was not clearly demonstrated, because I cannot remember even this supposedly completed act. And just because I woke up next to the dead woman and thereby was naked, and had put on a sperm filled condom, that does not mean that I have done that too. The semen must not have been mine - or maybe it is not a real sperm at all. Maybe someone came to me when I fell asleep, has covered me with the condom and the semen or something of similar appearance in it. Before that, I was still completely undressed, and placed next to the body. It was there next to me when I woke up, I was also so

shocked that I've actually done it. It is plausible, right? After knowing all these things, you are not going to come back to me, Rita? Stupid cow!
"Maybe the guy made me sleep using hypnosis or gave me something, and so has led me to do it," I push behind. And dub myself so secretly even as a coward. I should not tell her all these stupid things and instead of keeping it for myself, I could not control my thoughts.
"Yes, probably." She tries not to laugh while she is saying it.
"What now, you are going to help me?" I ask impatiently and now annoyed.
This will be my last request to her. Everything related to my future depends on her response now. If she helps me, would be great, if not, it is also fine.
The final resignation takes possession over me. My despair which has taken place in myself has degenerated into indifference. I just want that it stops, that it ends, no matter how it turns out for me in the end. My old life is only a memory anyway. Even if now should everything become better, even though nothing is as before. I am now a different person in a completely new life.
"Dirk, remember why I broke up with you that time?"
It comes with a question. How I hate that. Why is it always so difficult for women to answer with a simple 'Yes' or 'No'? Instead, a counter-question is asked, which also completely misses the point of

the overall subject. Because of the anger I feel, I do not remember that I previously came up short with another question. Is she copying me or what?

"Sure I remember it, do you think I lied to you all the time, because I never confessed my love to you , all these years, or is something like that becoming a problem ..." I ruefully answer her.

"That was not the only reason," she says in a regretful and downright cautious tone.

"What was it then? Was there another type? "

"No."

"Then?"

"I was afraid of you."

This is something new. I could expect anything but not this. These words hit me deep into the marrow.

"Why did you have fear of me? I do not know that I ever given you a reason for it. "

"You did not give me a reason, not directly anyway. It was your behavior that was always strange. "

"In which way?"

"You started to sleepwalk and during that you led soliloquies."

"I did what?" I ask in astonishment, although a statement about my "self-talk" was something that should not surprise me that much. But I have never expected it from someone with whom I was so closely linked, as with Rita. Actually only from people who do not like me and want to poke fun at me.

"You have done self-talk, at first only if you were asleep, but then I have caught you while you were awake. Or if we sat together on the couch and we saw a film, or in the morning at breakfast. It seemed to me as if you were far away, and did not perceive what is happening in reality, at the moment when we are together. Sometimes I felt as ... "she stops and takes a break before she continues talking," ... as if I am dealing and talking with another person. "

All this sounds so unreal, beyond my imagination. I cannot wait to hear what she says next. I ask her to continue.

"Your behavior was at some places completely different, you wanted to arm the people without any reason and that is something you did not do before. You were right tantrums over trifles. For example, once when we were shopping, an elderly woman was paying the bill with the coins at the grocery store, you became so upset and you freaked out because we had to wait for a while until she finished. You have actually made that woman cry. And how did you ever run away from the non-functioning reverse vending machines. I had eventually decided not to collect them anymore and to throw them better away. Sometimes I had to keep them secretly. Another tie, you have even knocked a little boy off his bike when he drove too close to you. I was really surprised when you started doing such things"

"What? I cannot remember those thing, "I note surprised.

"That does not surprise me. Because whenever I spoke to you about such actions, you did not know anything about them. "

"I'm sorry, but I ca not believe that it is truth," I make it clear.

I'd would like to remember such behavior. But I am just not willing to focus my thought on it. That's not me. I've always been nice - polite and courteous. I'm the cute boy next door, the goddamn prime example. And nice guys next door do not make old women cry and do not push children from their bicycles. Such guy will not start to argue with others for no reason, or run asleep around and chat with himself. About whom is she talking about?

"Believe me, because you've done it all ... Dirk, you got so scary. So scary that you scared me and that I had no choice but to separate myself from you. From your bloody confession apart. "

After she has said it, follows a mutual silence. What tons weighs heavily in the atmosphere.

"Dirk, I think you killed all these people," Rita says to me, and as she says it to me, I get an impression that it gently breaks me inside. But that does not help, because I did not kill anybody. And I also do not know what the whole thing is going now.

"No I have not. I swear to you, "I assure her while trying to convince her and to sound honest. I feel as if I am sitting on the dock and being condemned to life imprisonment at the moment. Although I am innocent.

"Dirk, you have them all on your conscience, I am convinced," she says, this time less friendly, but with unshakable conviction in her voice.

What she says there? What is she afraid of?

Anxiety?

This should be at once "the real reason"?

Afraid of me? Since she would carry this everything on her conscience too?

She caught herself lying behind her accursed door. Perhaps it is even, because she's scared! Oh yes, exactly.

Afraid to be loved. That's it! Only because all her previous acquaintances were namely so quickly brought to an end!

This stupid bitch!

I have lied for many years? I loved her for all these years!

I loved her, while she has closed her eyes to, to freely overdo it with others! She did not know that I love her? Oh, what a surprise! What a lie! That damned bitch crap - I was her best friend? I was probably best suited to bring her to New Year's Eve from the Reserve Bank, as the itching got worse! Who has here lied in fact, who has been abused downright? Me! Me, and no one else! The fool who was the stupid one, who has always been stupid one, and should stay stupid, that is me! The practice dummy who was there for a relationship incompetent whore, who made her two-year

puzzle, unfinished life image of her serial monogamy complete!
Because I love her, I lied to her! So - the physical affection of any horny whoremongers had yet been much better, right? Much safer, right?
I understand why this cursed door will not open. Oh yes, I understand.
Who knew that he was not beloved, that he was eventually needed to fix out everything after the other one left her, right? The one who was not beloved, cannot be left as well, right? At least not in the classic sense. But he has been able to convince her that she was beloved whenever she wanted him to do that!
Gradually everything is perfectly clear to me. Thanks Rita that your new filthy lies finally unmask your greasy, staged separation lie, you disgusting cunt.
The "best friend" in reality was being the 'real lover "for long time? How could you be hurt if you could not even love him, how could you be Rita honey? If you had to convince yourself that you are not beloved just because you actually did not know what that really was! How awful is the illusion of having everything in hand, and then losing it at once! When the lie of your best friend - his well-kept secret – has made all this to you which you have actually made to yourself and to others as well!
How bad must it have been for you if your own, well kept secrets you whisper at once: I, the liar,

am the whole your past.

The possibility of being able to leave, nourished all
their anxiety. That was it. And the only way to
eliminate this possibility was to leave those who
truthfully loved you, before they even would come
to an idea to do it. The door must be locked from
the inside - in the truest sense of the word. And
they must remain locked! Thus the delusion
remains safe.

This is all her anxiety. This is her whole unloved
life. This is Rita.

As she trembled when she learned the truth! As
her whole face was one big horror when her
mortal fear of my love froze her soul - with love in
it! Can she be killed by someone who has actually
loved her so much! Yes, this message has
abundantly been clear in her blue eyes. But
someone like that person was not there, right? He
was not allowed to enter the apartment. And she
was the only reason. Nobody else!

But what does it bring now?

She would stare at me while I am talking to her,
and then I would be gone. It would all happen in
in quiet way, which is actually much better - but
now I have to go without saying goodbye.

But I could not. I had to say goodbye to her! And I
used always to do it before I went. Everything was
taken from me. And I should be crazy now if I am

coming back now to get more of what she has never given to me.
But I have to take every chance.
Each, and even the smallest one.
I need to get in finally. If I need anything, then, that is it!

And she has to do something. She has to open this goddamn door finally.
She has to know that I'm not a murderer!

What should I tell her?

"Maybe everything what you said about me, is true. That I lead soliloquies and all other thing which you accused me for. But that does not mean that I am killing people. I am not crazy."

"Yes, you are," she answers.

"What makes you think so?"

"Because you're talking again with yourself."

Disappear Here.

"Because you're talking again with yourself."

I hear it loud and clear, but I do not want to admit
that she has just told me that, it does not want to
move into my cerebrum. What did she just say?
The hallway suddenly seemed tiny. I overcome it
by a feeling that I would fall into the void, like
right before falling asleep. To me it is very funny.
I have perhaps only imagined that Rita told me I
am talking to myself?

Did she, or not?

I am getting crazy or am I
already?

The words made me wake up, and now I stand
there and feel like being struck by lightning.
"Rita?" I shout and knock lightly
She does not answer.
So again: "Rita, Rita?"
Again nothing.
I call for her again, and press my ear to the door, at
least to hear anything. A motion, steps, a whisper,
(maybe she's not alone, tells me anything in my
head), or select the keypad of her phone (maybe
she calls so the police? was an idea of the voice in
my head), anything.
But nothing.
That makes me so angry that I start pounding with
my fists on her door and calling her continuously:
"Rita, Rita ... Rita, damn, give answer," I pull down
the doorknob, and experience a surprise that
petrifies me.
The door is not closed.
Why is the door unlocked?
She took the keys and has already opened the
door?
Did Rita opened me the door?
Is it the reason why she is not answering me?
Is this her way of telling me that I really should
just come in?
Or the door was never locked?
I gently push the door, it swings to maximum, and

then remains at one point. I can now see Rita's apartment. But there is no trace of Rita. I look directly into the living area of her two-bedroom apartment. Should I come in now, I'm standing right in her living room. It's all so messy, downright messy. A table lamp lying on the floor, and a chair. A small picture frame made of wood lying down on the ground, and it is integrated so that you could set the frame again without any problem. Individual garments are distributed everywhere, and the seat cushion of the sofa lying around there but at its place. All this does not fit to Rita, she is the neatest woman I have ever known. Something is wrong here. It almost looks as if something has happened, a battle, perhaps?
Was that possibly you?
I have literally to force myself to come in, something inside does not want me to do that, it wants to warn me, tell me: *Run better away. Far away. When you have gone through that door, there's no turning back. Although you can find out the truth about everything, but there is no turning back, be aware of that.*
I seriously take this warning, but at the same time it confuses me too.
Why should the events of the last hour been cleared here in Rita's apartment?
What Rita has to do with it?
Has the voice, which belongs to this comic Ben, Rita in custody and I am going to meet him?

Or he blackmails Rita?

Are the voice and Rita possibly under a blanket?

I do not know. But I need to know. The need to finally know the truth, to finally know what a sick game is played with me, is almost overpowering. My heart is pounding and hammering, so I can feel it even in the ears. I move slowly, every step I take is carefully considered, as if I would walk barefoot on broken glass. But I'm always ready to turn around and run away.

After I entered the apartment, I pushed the door a little so that I can come to the middle of the living room. I pick up the small wooden picture frame. I made it stand as it used to. The glass, which is located in the wooden frame, has a deep crack that runs across the top left corner to the lower right corner of the glass. Behind the glass hides a picture of Rita and me.

She is in my arms and we are grinning stupidly at the camera. We look happy, and we were. I know this and remember exactly where it originated:

In our first and only vacation together. It was on Madera. We were two weeks there and enjoyed the beach, the mountains, the wonderful climate, and the atmosphere. There was an incredible peace in which we only had time for us. The flight was a bit annoying as we unfortunately got seats in the tourist class, and then there was the near-crash while landing at Madera, anyway, it seemed to us that way. Fly never with this cheap suppliers in Berlin. It was really beautiful there. We took the entire tourist program, toured throughout Madera by bus, visiting the beautiful ancient churches, participated in a ride on a real pirate ship where I was terribly seasick. Due to the heavy swell, which momentarily gave the impression that we would capsize. We saw dolphins and a sea turtle and swam in a bay where the water was so clear that we could see the seabed. We had almost every day sex, several times. The nocturnal walks on the lighted beach were always the crowning statements of perfect days.

I put the photo frame, which I have picked up, back to its place back. Putting it as it was on the floor. So no one sees it, not even me. Let bygones be bygones, something tells me that in my head. And the voice that I am thereby imagining is vaguely familiar, but I cannot classify it.

Suddenly I hear a melody. Or rather a song, I know this song. It's Hammerhead by The Offspring. He comes from a cell phone lying on the coffee table. This phone seems damn similar. Shit, I think that's my phone!

How can it be here, I have thrown it on the highway? Bang, bang, it hammers in my head.

In my head, in my head sing The Offspring, and they're damn right. What's going on here? I go to the phone and take the call.

"Who's there?" I shout.

"It's me, your favorite voice," the voice is happy to answer.

"How do you ... Bloody hell, get my phone ... I ...

AHHH ... FUCK!" I have no words.

"Did you miss me?"

"Fuck you!"

"What kind of expression. Do you kiss your mother in the mouth? "

"Where's Rita?

"Always nice and slowly, one by one."

"Shut up, I mean, no, open up your mouth!"

"Well, what makes up your mind now?"

"Tell me where Rita is! What have you done to her?"

"The question should probably better be: What have YOU done to her?"

"What?"

"You have already understood."

"I did nothing to her!"

"Well then I have done nothing to her as well."

"Where is she?"

"I do not know, maybe in the bathroom? Why do not you check? "

He wants me to go to the bathroom - why he wants that? Is Rita really there, or lurking this bastard there? Is it a case or not, and why should Rita be in the bathroom? She has responded to me after all I said to her. And if she is there, then probably gagged in her power, or is there her body? There is only one way to find it out, but I do not want to go in there, I have a strange feeling that if I enter the bathroom now, there will be no turning back and nothing will be as it was.

I go to the bathroom and what I see there is a bath, which is filled with blood.
And there is Rita.
The phone falls down from my hand on the white tiled floor. Upon fall, it breaks down into its component parts and disappears soon after.
I want to scream, but my tongue get tied. Instead I hear an unspeakably loud, garish and yet dull beep tone, combined with a huge pressure. In fast motion, I see how the blood goes from dark red into a bright red, it becomes brighter and brighter, until it became clear water, which evaporates in the end. There is only the naked and lifeless body of Rita in the tub now, but it also resolves itself: I see how her skin slowly dissolves the body. Then I see the naked flesh, muscle fibers and veins. As her eyes emerge from the cave and then roll down. I see how the meat scraped from the bones themselves. Her skeleton and organs emerge. But organs disappear. Until her bare skeleton stays alone and expires to dust. The tub is suddenly empty.
You see only what you want.
Suddenly everything is so clear.
I can remember all my deeds now: The murder of Dennis, this unknown woman, who I hid on the highway. Mr. Becker, who was kind enough to help me, and had to pay for it with his life. I actually have all these people on my conscience. I am beginning to cry.
Did you finally get it?

The voice is my schizophrenic hallucination, and it
is talking to me.
*Have you finally understood that you are a very sick
young man who inflicts harm to other people? I am*
losing my mind
You did it already.
No, it cannot be true!
Come on, Dirk, let me finally come in.
Where then?
*In your head. I am standing in front of the door and
whispering to you. We have to merge together, so you
can really experience your deeds. No more memory
gaps, no black-outs, would not it be great?*
No, you stay outside!
*But there is no one who holds on you, I am only one
here.*
 Why? I do not understand that.
*You just have to understand that we reap what we sow.
I still do not understand?
You have created me.*
How?
*Through your fear. Your fear of everyone and every-
thing.*
Fear?
*Yes, your fear and your anger, your despair about not
knowing who your father is. He was never there for you.
He left you alone with whore of your mother, who has
always dragged another guy with. The fact is that you
were her shit and nothing more than a nuisance. That
your father left you alone before you were born, that he
does not even know that you exist. All this has created
me and made you what you are: A fearful, little loser*

full of self-doubt, with no trace guts. You're always running away from everything.

No, this cannot be.

Do not you remember how it was for you- for you as a class outsider? You were always an outsider, a looser as you says in the book. Every day you have been teased, beaten and ready in every way. From primary school to high school your teachers have made fun of you. No matter what you have done, you have never got recognition. Not even from your mother, although you've got so hard up.

Even though you were actually almost grown normally. Okay, you have been neglected from your mother and have never met your father, but you experienced lack of sexual abuse and no strict religious upbringing that led to excesses of religious conservatism. How could that be possible, your mother is the whore of Babylon himself? You have never dared to open your mouth. You have always said "Yes und Amen" to everybody. You have accepted everything without arguing, and then in your head you complains with yourself about it. In those moments you let me arise, and every time I become more and more a part of you. Has no one told you that it is like "mouth moves lips"?

You let everything go through you, and you were retrospectively angry. You enraged at your own wisdom. That you already started to talk to yourself before, in all these situations, in which you were so scared to do something about that, so you ALWAYS react on it. Over and over again, it is all in your head. When Rita finally showed her tits and allowed you to suck them, I could not stop myself.

It was already too late. It changed over time, and step by step I got a control over you.
When Rita left you, finally I could take you just for me. And now you'll never get rid of me!
No! No…
How many times have you wanted to be someone else? Someone, who cannot be so easily pushed around, someone, who has been respected by others, I am your revenge.
I am your revenge.
Did you finally understand that you have already begun to run amok and that nothing and nobody can stop you?
Go away and leave me alone!
It does not work anymore. If you have confronted yourself with your fear, I would not exist.
Simply disappear; I do not want to have anything with this.
Too late.
Cursed, no, damn it!
Come on; let me finally enter in your sweet, little brain. Stop defending yourself and you'll never be anxious and alone.
I begin to resign. One day, everyone will give up.
Well done, my boy. In the future you are going to do everything I command you.
I notice that the apartment door is going to open, and the door opens. A person comes in. I cannot see who it is. I see blurry and I have to vigorously rub my eyes before I can see anything.
It is Rita!
She stops on the spot looking at me in disbelief.
Rita? She is alive?

Yes, and that is our problem.

What do you mean?

You know what you need to do.

No.

Kill her.

I cannot do that!

Yes you can.

No, please let her live!

You know very well that if you do not kill her, I will do it.

I'm coming close to Rita, and she says to me: "Do not do anything to me, please Dirk".

The end is not over yet...

To bring all this to an end, there is only one
solution that remains.
I have to kill myself!
The madness that is taking place in my head is the
true life.
It is not too late to get rid of this madness before I
have to kill other people.
*But you cannot kill yourself, because you are too afraid
of doing it just like you were before.*
The voice is right.

End?

Epilogue

In this psychological thriller, you are pursuing a man who goes mad, whose main problem is his fear of conflict, getting into any contact with people. But before Dirk now condemn you; think again how you solve your conflicts! Do you immediately pack them, or possibly just like my protagonist Dirk - run from problems away? Dou you rather get them out of your life path, and try to forget them because you think that it is not so bad, and you think that everything happens because of that paralyzing fear that takes them over and makes them incapacitated?

How is it with monologues? Do you occasionally run some? Do you know or did you know someone who does it? Do you think it does not happen too often and that those are cray, and / or suffer from a multiple personality disorders, as it does Dirk?

Before you jump to conclusions, or condemn, I will give you a tip: Look at the people around you. Give yourself a little time. I mean not only family members, friends, or colleagues. Look at all of them!

Take a look to the people walking on the street, or while driving the car.

Go to a supermarket, stop in front of it and watch the people who are coming in and out.

Park your car on any parking lot and search for

people who move their lips, even though they are traveling unaccompanied.

You will be surprised that there are many people who are (even in public) talking to themselves.

But why they do that?

And would it be really so crazy when someone of us would do the same?